KALEIDOSCOPE

Complex set of events: a complex set of events or circumstances

Complex scene or pattern: a complex, colorful, and shifting pattern or scene

KALEIDOSCOPE

A CARLA MCCARTHY ADVENTURE

Gretchen Stone

iUniverse, Inc.
New York Lincoln Shanghai

KALEIDOSCOPE
A CARLA MCCARTHY ADVENTURE

iUniverse books may be ordered through booksellers or by contacting:

iUniverse
2021 Pine Lake Road, Suite 100
Lincoln, NE 68512
www.iuniverse.com
1-800-Authors (1-800-288-4677)

ISBN-13: 978-0-595-38745-8 (pbk)
ISBN-13: 978-0-595-83127-2 (ebk)
ISBN-10: 0-595-38745-4 (pbk)
ISBN-10: 0-595-83127-3 (ebk)

Printed in the United States of America

Acknowledgements

A warm thank you to the people who helped me, and also those who did not. It took love and support to get me going, and it took a stubborn desire to prove the rest of you wrong that kept me going.

Karen Haydu and Fran Blatnik both believed in me and without their support, I would still be floundering. Linda Haughton stepped in when I was tired and lent me her energy. Special thanks to the interesting women who were my inspiration: Ann, Kathi Kennedy, Bev Dale, Joan Smith, Marilyn, Marcia Fast, and Jane Smiley.

Sadly, the inspiration for My Sister's Bookstore is no longer part of our community. It is a loss felt keenly by women readers in Michigan. If you have a women's bookstore in your community, support it.

Location: Southeast Michigan
Cast of Participants

<u>China Jane</u> The taciturn owner of China Jane's, not the fanciest restaurant on the strip but one of the best and busiest. She is sometimes seen just before closing time, having a Tsingtao with the owner of the beauty shop.

<u>Tootsie Siegel</u> Owner of the Hair Boutique, she is frequently seen socializing instead of working.

<u>Nan Lawson</u> Montrose's first female Chief of Police. Her 'strictly business' demeanor does not encourage casual conversation or personal questions.

<u>Pete Brown</u> Owner of the Candid Times, he considers himself a liberal, but it is clear he hasn't gotten over his puritanical upbringing.

<u>Miriam Brown</u> A sad neurotic woman who has devoted her life to her son. She insists on helping him at the Times by answering the telephone and taking want ad orders.

<u>Carla Ann McCarthy</u> Co-owner of a blueberry farm in mid Michigan and the roving correspondent and assistant city editor at the Times.

<u>Abigail Carr</u> A British author visiting Montrose on her second American book tour.

<u>Laverne Stephenson & Shirley King</u> Owners of My Sister's Books, the second largest Women's bookstore in the Midwest.

<u>Ginger Harris</u> An independent bar maid with the face of an angel but some think there is more to her than meets the eye. The reputation she is most proud of is the ability to keep a secret.

Frankie Q. Black Former girl's high school basketball coach now divides her time working as a bouncer at the bar with Ginger and playing drums for a local jazz band.

Darilyn D'Angelo Owner and chef of a vegetarian restaurant. Charismatic, charming but some see her as enigmatic and cunning.

Maria Morgan The proprietor of The Italian Café, she lives life with gusto.

Belinda Norton The daughter of a preacher and the wife of a wealthy older man, she wants something more from life. Her money buys an open door to organizations that her background would close to her.

Introduction

Montrose is a pleasant American city not far from the Canadian border. It is your typical adolescent small town struggling with growing pains, a blemish or two, and a yearning to be in control of its own destiny. Long time residents proclaim their German and Irish heritage as proudly as they produce prolific candid snapshots of their grandchildren for visitors.

The narrow wooden homes had been outgrown and cast down to the next generation with honor more than once but are now in search of a new public persona. Upwardly mobile children and grandchildren who no longer valued living in the homes where their parents prospered traded up to the brick suburbs built by the UAW and CIO with money from General Motors and Ford.

An alternative community of artists, musicians, hairdressers, dog groomers and ethnic restaurateurs moved in. Certainly not hippies or flag burners but not quite mainstream either. They planted flowers and painted their mailboxes with rainbow flags or morning glories. Here and there around town, you may glimpse a backyard waterfall or spy a prolific pumpkin patch over a privacy fence.

The political atmosphere marches in step with the business community and the changing population. As feminist bookstores, tattoo parlors, and vegetarian restaurants gradually replace the five and dime, shoe repair shop, and fabrics store, the make-up of the city council, mayor's office and police department adapts.

In the nineteen seventies, Dutch Elm disease decimated the elm trees that had lined every street. The city eventually recovered and new trees grew. Today, thirty years later, Emerald Ash Borers are killing trees on every block again.

As you might expect, ethnic and cultural diversity flourishes in Montrose. People who live and work here are mostly good. A few are bad. Regardless of their education level, most residents generally have common sense. Unfortunately, for all, a few do not.

Ginger Harris
7:30 AM Thursday Sept 7, 2000

A wet kiss traveled across her cheek and ended in her ear before she was awake enough to resist. Instead of being annoyed, she laughed and gave the offender a hug. "Scotty, what would I do without you? Probably sleep till noon, wouldn't I? What a good boy. Come on, let's get up, and go out." Throwing off the rumpled blue sheets and cabbage rose quilt, she slipped into her robe and slippers and headed towards the aroma of Mr. Coffee wafting from her sunlit kitchen.

Buster was at the back door watching the pesky squirrels and birds and making plans to let them know it was his territory as soon as Ginger lets him out. "You're a good boy too, Buster. Nice and quiet until Mommy gets up. Good boy."

By the time she finished the pot of coffee, she had a good idea of what the day was going to be like. It was Thursday and tonight she was going to be helping at My Sister's Books for a few hours during the First Thursday event. She was looking forward to meeting Abigail Carr and hearing her read from her latest novel about an exclusive girl's school in England. Ginger's parents had sent her to boarding school when she was eight, but she behaved so badly, the school sent her home when she was ten, and that was the end of her private school education.

There was plenty of time to work in the yard for awhile before she needed to get ready to go and Buster needed some 'run and get the ball' time. The morning sun was pleasant, and fat yellow bees hummed contentedly as they busied themselves dividing their time between the fragrant blue blossoms of Bee Balm bushes and the Black-eyed Susan's. After a couple of hours, she made a glass of ice tea and settled down in a wicker lawn chair on the deck to read a few more pages of *Ethics for the New Millennium*. The Dalai Lama wasn't her traditional easy summer reading but Ginger had made a commitment to herself to read one serious book for every Dean Koontz or James Patterson thriller.

When her phone rang around two, she knew it would be Frankie checking in. That is what she loved about Frankie, and that is what she hated about Frankie. Sometimes their relationship felt reliable and dependable; sometimes it felt predictable and boring. Seven years was a long time to be adored.

"Hi, Frankie. Yes I'm fine, and you?"
"Just reading and playing with the dogs." Ginger gave Buster a rub behind the ears.
"Yes, of course I'm planning to be at the book store tonight. I couldn't let Laverne down, plus I am looking forward to hearing the speaker."
"Are you playing this weekend?"
"Ok, see you tonight…I love you too. Bye."

Sometimes Ginger thought it wouldn't matter what she said; Frankie took it for granted that everything was fine.

The next time the phone rang, she was surprised. Very surprised.

"What an unexpected pleasure to hear from you! I had no idea that you had my phone number."
"I would like to see you too."
"Of course I will, if you think I can help."
"Yes, you can count on me."
"Good, I'll see you soon."

Getting dressed was more fun than usual that day. Dusty Springfield and Tracy Chapman battled it out on dueling stereos as Ginger wandered from bedroom to den checking her wardrobe choices in every mirror in the house. After trying on a dark blue dress: "What was I thinking, Buster? This is awful!" Next, chocolate brown wool pants and a green sweater: "Way too autumnal for tonight." Sharply creased jeans and a button down white shirt: "Too lezzy, not really me." She eventually settled on a light blue linen pantsuit that promised to look feminine, be comfortable and flattering, if a little predictable.

Choosing a Dvorak concerto to keep the dogs company while she was out, she set the CD player to repeat, turned the volume down, and lowered all the blinds. The dogs were used to her going to work at night and didn't whine when she left early today.

When she pulled the car out of the garage, she could smell the sharp, sweet smell of autumn in the air. She was filled with a sense of well being, enjoying the anticipation of deja new. Not only did she expect to enjoy herself tonight, she was on her way to help a friend.

Brenda Cook Norton
7:30 AM Thursday Sept 7, 2000

She was wide-awake in an instant. There was never any need for an alarm clock in this house. As soon as the heavy front door closed, she instinctively knew she could get up. Today was a new day. She knew some of the things that would happen, but not all.

Autumn had always been a time for new beginnings. New schools, new clothes, sometimes new friends. Nine years ago, a new husband. Each year since, an anniversary trip in the fall to somewhere new. Somewhere she could relax and unwind, somewhere that would create the magic moment she and her husband had prayed for.

She no longer expected to come home pregnant. She was thirty, still not too old to have a baby, but after nine years of waiting, only her mother and her husband still expected her to keep trying.

In the last few years, her husband had seemed cold, distant. They had separate rooms now, but he still came to hers when he wanted, only to leave minutes later. Her disappointment became his only failure in life.

She grew up privileged but lonely. Her father was a Southern Baptist minister, and her mother stayed at home with Belinda and her two brothers. Being the preacher's kid was just one of the things that made Belinda feel different. From the age of five, she had refused to eat anything with meat in it. No matter how her mother pleaded and her father threatened, she stubbornly refused. Her father was so upset with her defiance he frequently threatened to "take his belt off to her." He lost his temper one night and harshly beat her across her scrawny back and legs. The next day her mother announced her decision to send her to boarding school.

By the time Belinda was sixteen, her father had decided upon a suitable husband for her. Jeremy Norton was a wealthy widower who served as a deacon in the First Baptist Christian Church. After his first wife died in childbirth, he spent the next dozen years making his fortune and didn't want to take the time to court a new wife. His generous tithes made up for the many services he missed and ensured the expansion of Pastor Cook's ministry.

Belinda's mother convinced her husband that their daughter should have an education before her marriage. A Bachelor of Arts degree in Women's Studies opened Belinda's eyes to many things in the world outside of the ingrained Baptist community she grew up in.

She stayed in touch with a few friends from college after she married. She was grateful to find kindred spirits when she joined a women's monthly reading group that promoted ecological responsibility as well as vegetarianism. She threw herself into recycling efforts in her upscale Rosedale Park neighborhood and bought cookbooks that promised *Vegetarian Meals for the Meat Lover in Your Life.*

Five years after her marriage, she rationalized her husband didn't love her any more, and she had an affair with Nikki Applegate. Nikki was a radical feminist activist and poet who earned her living as a midwife. She was at every rally for equal rights for women, every Democratic candidate, every labor union leader, and every anti-war demonstration. She could be seen marching at the head of Gay Pride parades in Chicago, Detroit, and Toronto every June.

For Belinda, it was the love she had yearned for. Nikki was not uncaring, but she was not the type to settle down. The affair lasted a year, in part because Nikki did not want to hurt Belinda and in part, because Belinda made so few demands on Nikki's time. When she told Nikki she was going to leave Jeremy so they could be together, Nikki panicked. She moved to San Francisco and took a job as the director at a Gay and Lesbian Health Center.

When the affair was over, Belinda reluctantly went back to her old life but she started making plans. Some day she would live the life she wanted. She'd had a bank account since she was twelve and deposited every Christmas gift, every birthday gift from her family. Long ago, she had convinced her family she preferred receiving cash on special occasions.

2:15 P.M When the phone in her room rang, she quickly picked it up.

"Hello, hello! I'm here! I'm so glad you called. I can't wait till tonight to see you."
"Can you leave early and go to the bookstore with me to meet Abigail Carr?"

"All right, of course, I understand. I will meet you at the usual time."
"OK, see you soon. Don't forget to unlock the back door for me."

7:15 PM Jeremy Norton lowered his big frame carefully into a hardback chair in his study. There was no dinner waiting for him but he didn't expect any tonight. He could hear the water running in his wife's shower and smell the mix of lavender soap and shampoo. When the water stopped, those scents were replaced with the familiar scent of the imported body lotion and perfume he always gave her on her birthday.

As he listened to the buzz of the hairdryer, he imagined her standing in her ivory lace lingerie with her head bent and her long dark hair tumbled around her face.

He didn't look up from the work on his desk when he heard her descending the stairs. He listened intently as her footsteps crossed the living room to his study, as she came to say good night.

"Jeremy?"

At the sound of her voice, he looked up at his wife. She seemed aglow, olive skin gleaming, wearing a dark brown, silk pantsuit, gold earrings, gold neck chains, bracelets. So much jewelry, he thought. Does anyone notice the gold and diamond ring? Her wedding ring?

"I'm leaving now. Don't wait up for me; I might be late. You know how these committee things are. No one can ever agree on anything."

He watched as she paused to select a coat from the hall closet. Of course, the zibeline. His wife cares very much about how she looks. One last look and she was gone.

Darilyn D'Angelo
7:00 AM Thursday Sept 7, 2000

The alarm clock was set to a Gentle Rain selection, which frequently caused at least one snooze button reset. This morning was not any different. The crisp linen sheets and cozy white cotton blanket promised ten more minutes of refuge and invited their guest to linger. The woman struggling awake from a deep sleep wondered, "*Where am I? What day is this?*" without caring very much what the answers were.

At 7:30, a second alarm shrilled from across the room, snooze button out of reach. "*Damn it, I may as well get up. I'm sure I have a lot to do today-I always do.*"

A glass of fresh-squeezed apple and carrot juices mixed with wheat grass, and a morning reality check with CNN news brought Darilyn fully awake by eight. The next hour was filled with aerobics followed by another hour of meditation and yoga.

A quick shower and she was out of the house by 10:30, on her way to Eastern Market. Today she was picking up a dozen new sauté pans and stainless steel woks she had special-ordered weeks ago from Magglio's Market. While she was there, she looked at the Wusthof Trident kitchen knives she has lusted after since she used them in London. There was a perfect place for a set of ten in her kitchen to go along with her new pans.

She took pride in selecting the freshest fruits and vegetables for her weekend menu from the outdoor market. Although it was late at the farmer's market, her regular vendors knew she would be there and have already set aside the daikon, sweet onions, tomatoes, and basil she always needed. It was nearly time for Michigan apples, and she hoped to find enough Jonathons to make an apple tart. This was one of the best things about having her own restaurant. She could choose what to buy and what to cook. She had found a treasure trove of the vegetables and grains she preferred to cook with in Michigan.

The afternoon was sunny and warm, much like her cooking school days in Provence. Two of her early cooking jobs were in London and Vancouver, both of which were too cold and rainy for her. Much to her dismay, she found the glum, gray days easily influenced her disposition, and her sadness showed up in her food preparation as well as her personal life.

The crisp, late summer day and the scent of fresh produce wafting through the air in the outdoor market created a delicious sense of well being that washed over her. She walked over to the fresh herbs, and stood there for several minutes picking up bundles of mint, rosemary, tarragon, and dill, inhaling their fragrance.

The trip to the market left her with a pleasant feeling of satisfaction. Her plans were coming together.

Without thinking, she put away the spinach and basil and stacked her purchases from Magglio's in a corner. She sat down at the butcher-block table with a freshly brewed cup of lemon green tea, and picked up the phone.

Where mystery begins justice ends.

—Edmund Burke (1729–97), Irish philosopher, statesman.

Carla McCarthy
Friday 9:00 AM Sept 15, 2000

No one doubts that the police have done their jobs. Suspects have been arrested.

The prosecutor performed her job promptly. Charges have been filed. Now I must do my job.

I looked through the bars of one of Montrose's two holding cells at someone I liked and respected, someone I had considered a friend.

As a reporter, I was trained to ask who, what, why, where and when, but this time, I only want to know why. I am here more as a friend than as a reporter. "How did this happen?" I asked incredulously. "I can't believe you would be involved in something like this."

She said, "I grew up always trying to do the right thing. Explaining how things went so wrong won't be easy. It all started so long ago. What started as friendship and loyalty got all mixed up with love and then lies, and I didn't know how to get out of it. I've carried with me for years a quotation from Sir Walter Scott that says it all." She reached for her wallet before she realized she doesn't have it. Then she recites it to me with a surprisingly strong voice:

"Oh what a tangled web we weave, when first we practice to deceive."

Spring passes and one remembers one's innocence.

—Yoko Ono

Barbara Jane Brown
Detroit
Spring 1953

Before my family moved to Michigan in 1953, our earnest young Baptist minister cautioned Dad that Detroit was an integrated city, which in the 50's meant Christian and Jewish. General Motors had offered my father a job, and we reluctantly moved from rural Missouri to urban Michigan in June as soon as school was out that year.

Feelings about Jews were intense that hot, dry summer. As we drove two lane highways across miles of Indiana cornfields, the country music on the radio was abruptly interrupted by an ominous news update. Julius and Ethel Rosenberg had been executed for selling the formula for the atomic bomb to the Soviets. We rode in silence for a few minutes before I started to cry. My little brother wanted to know why I was crying. Dad said they were spies, and they put our country in a lot of danger. Almost fifty years later, I still remember the exact words he said that day:

"What they did wasn't right. They deserved to be punished."

Ginger Harris
Montrose
Thursday 5:00 PM, Sept 7, 2000

'*The fewer people who see me in Montrose at five in the afternoon the better,*"
Ginger thought gratefully, as she easily found a parking spot in the lot behind
the restaurant. Her luck continued when she saw the back door was open so
she didn't have to walk around to the front entrance. "*Spending an hour or two
doing something that I want to do for a change won't hurt anyone. If I'm lucky, no
one will ever know I was here.*"

As soon as Ginger entered, her hostess came out from the kitchen smiling a
welcome. Taking Ginger's hands in her own, she kissed her cheek.

"It's nice to see you at my place for a change. I am glad you could make it
this afternoon on such short notice. You are the busiest woman in town. I'll bet
you are going to work at the bar tonight, too."

"You are right, but first I have to go to the book store to help Laverne in a
couple of hours. I'm glad I could come here first. Your idea of a Women's Community Center for Montrose interests me. I want to hear all of your plans."

"I make a mean Long Island, is that okay? It's a secret recipe for special
occasions."

Ginger followed willingly as the taller woman led the way to her private
office. The intrusive sounds of customers coming and going faded away as the
heavy door shut, and the small radio was tuned low to easy listening music.

"A cool drink sounds great," Ginger agreed. Dinner could wait; the thought
of food was not as enticing as getting to know this enigmatic woman better.

The afternoon hours gradually slipped away as they talked. At first, the conversation focused on the need for a women's center but quickly expanded. The
two women from different backgrounds were soon openly exchanging personal experiences and their thoughts about women's equality and the lack of
opportunities for women of all ages and circumstances. They were delighted

but not at all surprised when their opinions of current elected officials and the state of the country matched.

Evening shadows and a pleasantly melancholy feeling spread throughout their surroundings when the conversation turned to aging and relationships. By seven, when Ginger realized she would be late, she tried to call Laverne at the bookstore, but there was no answer. The conversation was the most enjoyable she had experienced in a long time, and Jane's tales about women's communities around the world had intrigued her. She hated to see the visit end. "Just one more glass and then I really do have to go." By eight o'clock, Ginger was sound asleep; curled on one end of the couch with her head on the worn but still plump armrest. Jane was pleased, but perplexed with her unexpected somnolent guest. She would have to change her plans for the evening.

"Abracadabra, dum dum dum!"

—Bedtime Story Classic-The Little Lame Prince

Barbara Jane and Mimi
Detroit
Summer 1953

We met when she was six and I was eight. She was pounding loudly on our front door. I opened the door with some trepidation, expecting an angry neighbor or maybe even a policeman complaining about our moving van blocking the sidewalk. Instead, there stood a tiny girl with a feathered hat on, and a fragrant cinnamon coffeecake thrust out at me.

"I'm Mimi and I live next door and my Mother said you should have this." The words rushed out in a lilting singsong, as though she would forget what to say if she didn't let them out quickly enough. Her big brown eyes met mine with a look that implied we shared a secret.

It was my second day in Detroit, and she was the first girl I had met outside of Missouri. I remembered what our minister told us. "You will probably meet Jews in your new neighborhood," he advised my family in a hushed tone as we filed out of church together. "Big cities like New York, Chicago, and Detroit all have a lot of Jews."

I wondered if Jews wore pink hats like the one that Mimi wore. The feathers covered her long, dark curls, and the pink, knee high socks matched.

I soon learned that Mimi dressed up for everything special, and everything was special to her. Her Welcome Wagon Committee duties that day were a very special event for her. "My parents have been praying for a family with children to move in. The Bennetts used to live here but they retired and moved up north."

I looked down at her curiously. "Don't you have any brothers or sisters?"

"Just me, but sometimes Peter Cottontail comes to visit," she replied in a very grown-up manner as though Peter Cottontail was a real person.

She was an only child, and her parents indulged her love of fantasy and make-believe. During that first summer, she wore red nail polish on her fingers and toes every day and smoked candy cigarettes. When her Aunt Irene said she adored little girls with rosy cheeks, Mimi snuck her Mother's lipstick out of her purse and enlisted my help to draw roses on her cheeks.

That was the problem. No matter how ridiculous the idea was, I couldn't say no to her. My father was upset with me when I let Mimi cut off my long blond braid just a week before school started. She wanted the hair to make a tail for Peter Cottontail, her aunt's Manx kitten. When Aunt Irene caught us trying to use Band-Aids to attach the new tail to the screaming cat, she ended that project quickly, but my hair has never grown that long again. I think my Mother was secretly relieved not to have to braid it every morning, and I liked the freedom short hair gave me. Dad eventually stopped talking about it, but I don't think he ever forgot it.

See, that was the thing. Mimi's ideas may have seemed crazy, but some good usually came out of them. She lived in a fantasy world where unicorns were possible; *Step on a crack and break your Mother's back* was a real threat. The most powerful secret spell we had those summers in Detroit was "*Star Bright, Star Light, First Star I see tonight, wish I may, and wish I might, have the wish I wish tonight.*"

Sitting barelegged on the fence behind the garage, we would watch the sun slide between distant houses before it dropped out of sight. Listening to the radio, and waiting for the stars to come out seemed like enough to do at the end of a busy day. Our parents could see us back there, and sometimes they wouldn't call us to come in as soon as the streetlights came on.

"Oh look, Barbara Jane! There's the first star! Make a wish."

"Okay, I wish Miss Barr, my English teacher, would adopt me, and if I can't have that, I wish they would let girls play football at Mumford." Leaning back and looking at the darkening sky, I always added, "And I wish my Father would let me drive his Corvette. Now, you say."

"Star Bright, Star Light, I wish RJ could be the Little Prince and take me for a ride on the Magic Flying Carpet."

No matter how many times I tried to get Mimi to make a different wish, she never would. She changed her mind about everything else in her life, but she never stopped hoping to have a ride on that flying carpet with RJ.

Carla McCarthy and Abigail Carr
Montrose
Thursday 6:00 PM, Sept 07, 2000

My dinner date came striding across the restaurant in knee-high leather boots as though she is looking for a horse to tame. I wonder for a moment if she was going to attempt to put a saddle on me and smile at the picture that creates. Instead of the firm handshake I expected, she holds my hands as though she is protecting them from something. As we make our introductions, I don't have to look up, but if I don't I find myself looking at the large silver ornament balanced at the hollow of her throat on a thin, almost transparent silver chain.

"Hullo, I'm Abigail Carr. You must be the woman who promised me a good meal and a glass of wine. In return for which I am to give you a chat. Doesn't seem quite fair, does it?"

"Carla McCarthy, girl reporter. Perhaps it depends on what we chat about," is the best I can come up with on such short notice. Her thick, cropped dark hair makes me wish I had gotten the haircut I needed two weeks ago instead of spending the money on a new pair of Ferragamo shoes.

"Any relationship to the McCarthy who wrote *Don't Cry Mama*? I think her name was Carla too."

I'm not sure how to answer. Tonight I want to do the interviewing. My one moment of fame is long over, and although the residual checks still come in, I don't want to answer questions about why I haven't written anything else in fifteen years. It's too embarrassing to admit I have a terminal case of fear of success.

"It's not such a common name, but I doubt she would be hidden away here in suburban Montrose. I'm sure with all of her money; she is living a life of leisure somewhere, not doing interviews for a local paper. All of my friends loved that book."

Well, that put me in my place. I almost admitted it, just to see the look on her face.

Dinner tonight promises to be much more interesting than my usual predictable restaurant reviews. When I telephoned Abigail Carr a week ago to schedule an interview, I had forgotten how slow the service is at Vegelina's Restaurant. The proprietor, Darilyn D'Angelo, does all of the cooking and most of the serving herself, and tonight she wants to talk, too. Some other night I might have appreciated the owner taking a personal interest in our meal, but not tonight.

Not that I can blame her, Abby's English accent is a delight to listen to. Listening to her talk about the scandals in the equine world of dressage makes me want to go right out and buy her previous book, even though it didn't make it onto my must read list when it was first published. The new book she is promoting is about the mystique of a private girl's boarding school. Before the night is over I will have my own autographed copy, and I can't wait to read it. The advanced classes I took in public high school didn't give me many chances to form close friendships with any of my classmates before I graduated at sixteen. Boarding schools are a subject I have always had a secret and prurient curiosity about.

"I love the necklace you are wearing. I've never seen one quite like it." I don't mind paying a compliment to get people to open up and tell me about themselves.

"It's a Labrys. I've had this one custom made for me."

"I don't mean to stare but it is quite unique. I notice it is three dimensional, is it a butterfly symbol?"

"No, it is a double bladed axe, an ancient symbol that was worn by the original Amazons. It symbolizes strong and independent women who make their own choices."

"Well I wasn't too far off. Many women I know in twelve-step programs wear butterfly jewelry as a symbol of their personal transformation."

Darilyn brings our salads to our table herself and waits to see if we approve of the baby spinach, walnuts, and pomegranate seeds. "I tried something new. Let me know if you don't like it." She hovers around waiting for us to try the salads, and I wish she would go back to the kitchen. I sense she is looking for approval for herself more than for the salads. I don't want any distractions while Abigail is willing to talk about herself.

"I have wanted to write about private boarding schools for girls for a very long time," she begins. "Most everything that is published is so bloody pedantic or inordinately prurient. Depends on your point of view, I suppose." She hesitates briefly to see if I will laugh.

"My intent was to expose more accurately the daily realities, the lifelong relationships that are formed during the years when young women are first away from their homes and families. Often the ties that are formed during those adolescent years are closer than any others throughout life."

"Expose? So there are—" Before I can finish my thought she quickly responds.

"Did I say expose? Perhaps I should have said disclose. My intent is not to stir up any old scandals or create new ones."

"Did you go to a boarding school?"

She nods. "We were allowed to bring our horses, and there were very suitable equestrian facilities there. My older sister and I both went to Queen Ethleburga in England. It is a very well thought of school near Leeds, where I grew up."

It is a little disconcerting the way she keeps looking at my open shirt. She isn't afraid to meet my eyes, daring me to call her on it. Her alabaster skin pinks up on her cheeks, and I wonder if it can be a blush, but I decide it is more likely another type of reaction. She is a very interesting woman, and her brashness intrigues me more than it puts me off.

"Any life long friendships from your time there?" I ask curiously jealous.

After a pause, she replies with a slow grin, "Yes, I guess you could say that."

❦   ❦   ❦

Abigail seems pleased with Darilyn's specialty, lemongrass soufflé with flat noodles, and we are ready to leave, when Maria comes in. The glaze over her startling sky blue eyes tells me she has been drinking early tonight. Maria Morgan is the owner of the Italian Gardens restaurant across the street from Vegelina's. "Carla! I thought I saw your car in the parking lot." She is speaking to me, but looking at Darilyn and Abigail.

Her belligerent tone implies she is also feeling a little jealous. She and I go through this any time either of us start seeing someone new. Although it was a long time ago, Maria and I dated for awhile back in the casual seventies. It was just a couple of nights that started at the Palais Bar and ended up in the roomy backseat of her black and white Chevy Impala one memorable night on Belle Isle. The pulsating fountain lights at the Scott Fountain in the center of the island made making out seem more peccantly intense than it really was. We were both young, and the thought of passing cars catching us in their headlights was more intoxicating than the mixed drinks we'd had at the women's bar on Detroit's east side.

Urban renewal inevitably won the battle and the bar was torn down, but Belle Isle is still here and so are Maria and I. Amazingly enough, Belle, Maria, and I have all managed to age to a certain desirable stage of ripeness. She may not have recognized Abigail Carr as the celebrated British author, but she knows competition when she sees it.

"Hi, Maria. What are you doing here? Just checking out the competition or did you come over for a take-out?" I am hoping she will recognize my weak attempt at humor and react accordingly.

"The question should be, what are you doing here?" Her reply is made without any hint of a smile. Apparently, she didn't get my joke.

"Oh no, here we go again," I think, but I know better than to say it out loud if I have any hope of diffusing the situation. Maria leans over the table and peers into my nearly empty teacup.

"So, you're serving wine now Darilyn? I hadn't heard that this dump got a permit. Maybe I should give the Liquor Control Board a call and just check for myself. You know, as a concerned resident and business owner."

Darilyn apparently isn't going to defend herself, which seems to inflame Maria even more. This is turning more into a brouhaha about the business competition and less about me. I should be relieved but I'm not.

"If you are trying to steal my customers, you aren't going to get away with it. You'll be sorry you messed with me." I had forgotten how strident she could be when she feels threatened. "I'll see to it that no one comes in here ever again."

With that, she glares at me for what feels like a long moment. After blustering that she will put Darilyn "out of business for good!", she flounces out with a menacing backward look at me.

I reluctantly follow her outside and try to calm her down. "Maria, darling, you know you will always have the best Italian restaurant in Montrose. No matter who else moves in, you are officially the Italian Queen. All Darilyn has is one mediocre red wine that she bottles herself, and she is only serving it in tea cups to personal friends until she can get a license."

"So, now you and the Dago are personal friends? I should have known I couldn't trust you, Carla Ann McCarthy! You have never cared about me or how I feel."

I want to laugh. This is so ridiculous, but I know that will only make it worse. I tell her "No, no, you've got it all wrong. Darilyn is only trying to impress the woman I am having dinner with. Abigail Carr is an author who is here from London. She is in the states for only a few weeks for a book tour. She is doing a book signing at My Sister's Books tonight."

When I attempt to grab her hand, Maria starts to stomp away, so I calmly tell her a big lie. "Abigail's agent told me she was a strict vegetarian. That is the only reason I brought her to Darilyn's instead of your place."

"Really? H-m-m-m I shoulda known something was going on between them. Darilyn is like a cat in heat. She was coming on to me until I made it clear I wasn't interested in her skinny ass. That spiritual type is so phony and tell her I said her tofu is phony too."

Somehow, this ludicrous exchange appeases her, and when she sees two car-loads of potential customers looking for a parking spot on her side of the street, she swaggers over to direct them to the lot behind her café.

❧   ❧   ❧

When I come back, I try to apologize to Abigail and Darilyn for Maria's erratic behavior. "I'm so sorry Maria is such a pain in the ass. She will forget all about this by tomorrow."

Darilyn's extremely pale skin is flushed, and she looks upset, but Abby seems mildly amused as though unpleasant encounters with angry women are something she is accustomed to.

Since she has been in town, Darilyn hasn't joined any of our loose knit community social events. I am not aware that she has made any public signs of being a lesbian, but even coming out as a Democrat would have gotten some doors opened for her in this election year. Most of us who have been around for a while would welcome someone new at our Friday night poker parties and occasional Sunday afternoon movies, but Darilyn so far has not been included. I am not sure if no one has asked her or if she just isn't interested in making friends. If one of the single women within our coterie has asked her out and gotten turned down, it isn't something they would have talked about to me.

I feel so bad about Maria's behavior tonight; maybe I should invite her to come to First Thursday with us. There is always a nice mixed crowd, and she can get to know some of the "regulars."

"Darilyn, could you close up early tonight and come to the book store with us to hear Abby read from her book? We would love to have you come with us." I hesitated before adding, "Trust me, I know Maria. She won't be there. She'll be watching the cash register at her place until she closes at midnight."

She tilts her head as though she is seriously considering my offer. "Thanks, but I'm not worried about Maria. I know her type—bark is worse than her bite, right? I need to stay here and close up. I'll be alone for the rest of the night. Darcy is scheduled to leave at nine. School night, you know. Sorry, maybe some other time?"

Darcy, the seventeen-year-old dishwasher who doubled as a bus girl on slow nights, was the only help Darilyn had in the kitchen during the week when things were slow. Hearing her name mentioned, the teenager comes out from the kitchen.

She starts clearing away our empty dishes. "Do you know how lucky we are to have Miss D'Angelo in Montrose? She was the chef at the Globe in London and at a four star restaurant in Vancouver!" It is clear the pretty, young brunette adores her boss. "Darilyn is going to teach me her cooking secrets so I can be a great chef like she is."

Darilyn looks pleased but manages to sound irritated. "Darcy, I'm sure they do not care in the least where I worked before I came here."

"Oh, but I do," Abigail speaks up. "My home is near London and I've eaten at the Globe several times. The food there is quite nice." She takes one last hopeful sip from her tea cup before surrendering it to Darcy.

Looking at my watch, I know we have to go or Laverne will be having a stroke. The bookstore has been advertising Abigail's visit and selling her books with the promise of having them signed by the author for weeks. I'm not surprised when Darilyn looks relieved that we are leaving.

Darilyn unexpectedly hugs both of us good-bye, and I wonder how a woman so thin could feel so sensual. There are breasts and hips there among the skin and bones. She smells familiar like autumn apples with vanilla and cinnamon.

Barbara Jane
Detroit
Summer, 1953

In our middle-class neighborhood of brick homes and green lawns, friend-ships among the children were encouraged while dating among the teenagers was not. Mom and Dad wanted good schools for us and kids to play with who wore shoes every day, not just to school and church. When they found the two-story home at the top of a hill near a Methodist church with a public library only three blocks away, they put down a deposit. The Eisenbergs, Seigels, and the Steins were all good neighbors and if there had been a slight dip in prop-erty values, it was erased when the realtors saw the streets being swept and the windows sparkling.

Corvettes made their debut the first year the Brown family lived in Detroit. That same year Dad came home with a new car. "The car is my present to myself," he explained to RJ and me. "General Motors sold it to me at a big dis-count, a special employee price." Of course, after hearing that about a dozen times, RJ and I started calling Dad's employer Generous Motors.

Even after Dad bought the white Corvette convertible, we still rode in the dependable Nash Rambler that we had come from Missouri in. It was dark green and the back seat was big enough for two pillows and a blanket when we were out after my bedtime. On summer nights when it was too hot to sleep, Mom and Dad would take us to the drive-in. If it was on Saturday night, we could bring Mimi along. RJ would fall asleep on the back seat as soon as the main feature came on unless it was a cowboy movie. Mimi and I usually stayed awake even if she had to pinch me. Our favorite was Marilyn Monroe in *Moga-mbo*. Dad agreed with us that she was the most beautiful woman in the world, unless of course Miss Elizabeth Taylor might have that title.

No one else in our neighborhood had a sports car. Sometimes Dad took me to the Texaco station with him on Saturday mornings. George checked the oil, cleaned the windows (which Dad always said were already clean), and pumped the gas. I pushed the buttons on the Wonderbar radio looking for a good song until Dad threatened me if I didn't sit still he would take me home and bring RJ next time. One Sunday, Dad drove me all the way to Flint with him so we could see where workers built Corvettes by hand. The only thing I didn't like about the car, was that it was a two seater so we could never bring Mimi along. Dad told our neighbors a Corvette might be made out of plastic, but it was going to change the way America built cars. His motto was, "If it is good for General Motors, it is good for America."

Loyalty was important to my Dad.

When I discovered a brand new magazine called TV Guide at the corner dime store with Lucille Ball on the cover, I used my allowance to buy it for my mother. She carefully cut out Lucy's picture and put it in a frame on the wall next to my grandmother's picture. A new 20-inch Muntz television sat in the corner of our living room across from the long mohair couch. "This television is for your mother," Dad told me and RJ so many times we would roll our eyes when he started. Mimi and I made Jiffy Pop on the kitchen stove while the TV warmed up, and we watched *I Love Lucy* sitting on that comfortable old couch with my mother every Tuesday night. I loved it when we all snuggled under the afghan Grandma had sent along to remind us of her and keep us warm up north.

RJ's favorite show was *Superman*. We were all amazed when Lois Lane showed up driving a Nash that looked just like our car. On Saturday nights, Mimi's parents came over for dinner and stayed to watch Milton Berle and Arthur Godfrey's talent show. Dad made milkshakes for the rest of us, but he would usually have a beer. RJ and I always insisted Dad was a better singer than anybody on the talent show was. We would plead and plead for him to sing at least one song. Our favorite song in those days was "Your Cheating Heart." I was so proud of him when he sang that song, I told him he was as good as Hank Williams any day.

Your cheating heart will make you weep
You'll cry and cry and try to sleep
But sleep won't come the whole night through
Your cheating heart will tell on you
When tears come down like falling rain
You'll toss around and call my name
You'll walk the floor the way I do
Your cheating heart will tell on you

When Mama told Mimi and me that Mr. Williams died the very day after he made that record, I wondered if he died from a broken heart.

Cheating seemed like a very bad thing in 1953.

Carla McCarthy and Nan Lawson
Montrose
Thursday early evening, September 7, 2000

"Tell me about Laverne and Shirley. What are they like?" Abigail seems pleasantly surprised to realize she can stretch her long legs out in the roomy passenger seat of my old DeSoto. She says it reminds her of a London taxi, and I can't tell if that is a good thing or if she is only teasing.

Pausing at the solitary red light we will pass tonight, I try to evade the question. "Oh, there is way too much to tell during the short ride to the bookstore."

"Start now and you can finish later," she demands as though she is accustomed to getting her own way.

"Since you put it that way," I said with a smile. "I've known Laverne Stephenson since she was teaching English literature to high school freshmen at Mumford in Detroit."

"So, she is a teacher. What about Shirley? Did they teach together?"

"That was long before any of us met Shirley King. That is not her real name, by the way."

"Now that is curious! Why did she change it? What does she have to hide?"

"As far as I know—nothing. It's an interesting story though. Not many people can remember what Shirley's name originally was. The year she moved to Michigan, she met Laverne at a teacher's conference in Lansing." I am already looking for a parking spot behind the book-store.

"That year they went to a Halloween party at the Roostertail Supper Club dressed in Laverne and Shirley costumes," I continued as we get out of the car. "Everyone started calling them Laverne and Shirley as a joke, and it has stuck."

"So, they are just friends?" Abigail doesn't give up easily, I am beginning to see.

"It's not easy to get them to talk about the past or their relationship. They are very private people. Some people think they are lovers and some think they are just friends and business partners. If you want to know the real story, you'll have to ask them."

As we get out of the car, I hear a little whine come from the engine. These short drives are hard on an old car. They just get warmed up and then you turn them off. It doesn't seem fair. The wind is starting to pick up and there are dark clouds on the horizon; it looks almost like snow, but it is months too soon.

Laverne greets Abigail and me with open arms held out for a hug before we are even in the door.

"I'm so glad you both could make it tonight. Come in please. There are some hors d'oeuvres and wine. Help yourselves," is her standard greeting to everyone.

I wonder if she is glad to see me, or if she is just relieved that Abigail Carr has actually shown up on time and sober. "Laverne, is Ginger here yet? I want to introduce her to Abigail"

Her hostess smile fades temporarily. "Carla, you'll have to look for her. I can't keep track of everyone. She was supposed to be here over an hour ago," Laverne is obviously on edge trying to ensure the evening goes smoothly.

"Who is Ginger? I love that name, I once had a cocker spaniel named Ginger."

We both laugh. Abigail is filled with curiosity; it must be the writer in her. I am the same way.

"Ginger is one of my best friends. She works at Les Girls, a popular woman's bar. She has been their bartender since they opened seven years ago. Now that I'm working at the Times, I don't get to the bar as often as I used to, so I count on seeing her here."

"A bartender? That surprises me." Abigail has mastered the art of the raised eyebrow. "I would have thought your friends would be more the cerebral type."

"Ginger is very bright. She could do anything she wants, but she enjoys her job at Les Girls. She has had the same job along with the same girlfriend for seven years. I've been having a midlife crisis during those same seven years, a different job, a different girl friend every couple of years. She helps me see there is hope for me yet. Her stability is important to me. I know I can always count on her."

As we circle the room, I point out a hand painted sign from the island of Maui hanging on one wall, which reads, "WELCOME TO LAVERNE AND SHIRLEY'S." Depending on your personal point of view, the bright pelicans, palm trees, and colorful sunsets can be construed either as a celebration of their relationship or just a colorful acknowledgement of their business partnership. Under the sign is a table with red wine, and Abigail adroitly snags a glass for each of us. "Your chum works here too?"

"No, she doesn't really work here. She helps out for a few hours during First Thursday events and occasionally on Sundays when the girls want a long weekend away." I'm sounding more defensive than I need to. My choice of friends is my business. "Ginger finds it hard to say no to anyone who asks for her help."

Those of us who had known Laverne since her teaching days in Detroit were surprised the first time we walked into the bookstore and saw Ginger behind the cash register. It's obvious that she is more a trusted friend than just a customer or employee. Laverne is very careful about who touches her money.

"Do her bartending skills actually cross over to book selling? She must be a different kind of bartender than I am used to," Abby admits sardonically with a half smile.

"Oh, most definitely. She is a natural at selling books even without the incentive of tips. Everyone thinks they are on Ginger's Top Five list, including me. If they gave awards for flirting, she would have a mantel full. She's had the opportunity to perfect the art during many years of serving drinks to unattached and lonely women."

"So, she is a flirt? Now I am beginning to see why she works at a bar and here also. She is looking for an adventure. I can't wait to meet her and see if I make it onto her Top Five list."

"I didn't mean to give you the wrong impression. The truth is, Ginger has been dating Frankie Q. for years. Frankie sat in on drums with the house band the night they met at Les Girls." It feels like I am still defending Ginger. "Frankie fell head over heels at first sight; it took Ginger a little longer."

"You didn't listen, reporter" Abigail retorts reproachfully. "I said she is looking for an adventure, I did not say 'she is looking for love.' The two things are very different, in my opinion."

An amazing number and variety of people have found their way to My Sister's Books since their first open house last year. The business was failing only a few years ago, an unkempt little bookstore with too many gaps on the sagging shelves. The two women took early retirement and gambled their savings to buy the place. Their creative energy along with hard physical labor has transformed My Sister's Books. Now it is the second largest bookstore east of the Mississippi specializing in the women's marketplace.

The open house was so successful; they decided to repeat it one Thursday each month. That's how First Thursdays was born. It's clear that both women love to throw a party. Each month is different with live music, poetry slams, and book signings interspersed with wine and cheese tasting parties, and even political discussion panels that I adore. I would never run for political office, but I am intrigued by the process. Laverne and Shirley haven't forgotten the importance of being good community citizens either and one Saturday afternoon each spring they sponsor a free community health screening for children and seniors.

I always check here first when I need to buy a birthday gift. They have expanded to sell not only the books and periodicals you would expect in a bookstore but also posters, DVDs, and hand picked gift items. The shelves along one wall are overflowing with videos and music CDs. Items they carry are unique but affordable. A boxed pair of martini glasses with tall stems encircled with rainbow threads was on sale after Christmas last year for only ten dollars.

People are coming in the front and back doors in twos and threes, and the store is rapidly reaching what would be the legal occupancy limit if this were a bar or a nightclub. It's noisy and the telephone behind the counter keeps ringing. More people have come tonight than I expected for a book signing. My Sister's Books is getting a reputation for plentiful, if cheap, red wine and Laverne's crab dip at these Thursday soirees, but it is also a good place to meet people. There are not enough chairs so people are milling around, no one seems interested in buying any books, and I hope this is not going to be a money-losing event for the "girls." I am one of the few people who know just how tight things are for the retired teachers. The phone keeps ringing incessantly but no one bothers to answer. "Will someone get that telephone, PLEASE?" No one pays any attention to my plaintive request.

I catch sight of Shirley limping towards the counter. When her years as a physical education teacher caught up with her, she needed surgery on her knee. She delayed for years but Laverne convinced her to relent last summer. Her recovery was more difficult than either of the women expected and she hasn't been able to put in as many hours at the store as before. They don't have any trouble finding part time help, but most of them are kids who don't want to work very hard for minimum wages. One precocious high school drop-out seemed to have potential until the WNBA lured her away from quiet little Montrose. The last any of us heard from her was a post card she sent to Shirley from somewhere on the road. Her new career traveling with a basketball team gave her perks Laverne and Shirley couldn't offer at the bookstore.

Across the room, I can see Abigail's head above the crowd. Her left arm is being firmly clutched by Laverne as she is led around the packed room for hasty introductions, so I don't need to worry about her for the moment.

I continue making the rounds chatting with the regulars. While introducing myself to some of the newcomers who are here to check out the politicians tonight, I keep looking for Ginger.

Nan Lawson is here out of uniform, which is unusual for her. Montrose's handsome Chief of Police is always aware of her public image. She is the commanding officer in charge of more than sixty police and civilian employees. They all have friends, families, and neighbors who are curious about the small town's first female police chief. It is safe to say she is the most recognizable woman in Montrose as well as one of the most private.

I've always admired her style and her perseverance. She worked her way up during more than twenty-five years on the force in the days when being a woman in a public position was unusual. In '87, not long after she earned her degree, she received a promotion to sergeant. Five or six years later, she was promoted again, this time to lieutenant. If there was any pressure on her to marry, she resisted it. Through the years, we have made a few mutual friends and have shared some good and some bad times. All of her close friends know Nan is a lesbian but of course, she is very discreet in public. A long-term relationship with her college sweetheart broke up five years ago when Kim got tired of living in the closet. Since then, Nan has had an occasional fling while she is on vacation in San Diego or during Women's Week in Provincetown but nothing serious. She is a good-looking woman, and if people want to assume she is married to her work, that is okay with her.

"Nan, my friend. Keeping an eye on the crowd or just socializing?" I asked, hoping I sound interesting enough to engage her in some casual conversation.

She hands me one of the two glasses of red wine she is holding and smiles. "Hello, Carla. I could say the same to you. Looking for a story or just looking?"

"I'm always looking for a story. I would love to interview you," I banter with her, but somehow I'm sure she knows I'm serious. "What a scoop that would be for the Times. You are one of a rare breed of women who actually knew what you wanted to do when you were nineteen."

With a twinkle in her blue eyes, she challenges me, "Are you saying I have a one track mind, or just that I don't know how to do anything else?"

"You know you impressed the hell out of me when we first met at Wayne and I found out you were already in the Montrose Police Department."

Taking a sip from her glass she reflects, "You were having a lot more fun than I was in those days. I was walking the beat. Nobody remembers those days any more."

"Those night classes at Wayne State were not so much fun either. I was taking business and journalism at night and interning at the Detroit News during the day."

"Don't remind me! That was the early 80's while I was working on my degree in criminal justice at night and walking the beat during the day! I wonder how my life would have turned out if I had switched my major to English lit when I had the chance. I might be living in a loft in Bricktown writing poetry now."

"You were already a police officer when we were both still teenagers. I was trying to decide if I should join the Peace Corps or write the great American novel while you were keeping the streets of Montrose safe."

"But you did write the great American novel. I know because I still have seven autographed copies of it. They make great presents, especially when I can tell someone the author is a friend of mine."

"That was luck, followed by years of picking blueberries. It wasn't that I always knew what I wanted to do. I just happen to like to write."

"Maybe I knew what I wanted then, but the older I get the more I wonder what else is out there. That loft doesn't sound so bad right now," she muses in a rare reflective mood as she drains her glass.

"Believe me Chief, you can have anything you want if you want it badly enough." I had just time enough to say before Shirley's announcement that Abigail was going to read interrupted us.

Barbara Jane and Mimi
Detroit
Autumn, 1953

Mimi was always at our house in those days. Mother didn't seem to mind. She said she was going to buy bunk beds for us but she never did. Mimi loved to sing, and she and my Mother would harmonize on silly songs while they peeled potatoes or made pie dough. They drove me crazy singing, *"How much is that doggy in the window, the one with the waggily tail? How much is that doggy in the window? I do wish that doggy were mine."* When they both started singing *"ARF ARF,"* I would leave the room.

Mimi never came over on Friday evenings. She had to stay home to light the menorah candles for dinner. Dad would take us to GillyGates for fish and chips on Friday so Mom didn't have to cook. A shiny tableside jukebox was next to every red vinyl booth. We all took turns putting nickels in to hear our favorite songs.

When we got home, that was my special time with Dad. RJ and Mom would play Monopoly sitting at the kitchen table until nine. Dad and I stayed up until eleven to watch *Friday Night Boxing Live! From Madison Square Garden in New York City.* My favorites were Kid Gavilan and Rocky Graziano, even though Dad tried hard to convince me Jersey Joe Walcott was the best fighter we would ever have the honor of seeing.

I wanted an exciting name like Jersey Joe. Barbara Jane was such a boring name. My parents let Bobby change his name to RJ when we moved to Michigan, and I wanted a new name too. During the World Series that year, I announced I wanted to be called Whitey Ford. When my parents stopped laughing, they explained that the first-born child of a General Motors employee could not be called a Ford of any color. I expected that, so I settled for my second choice, Yogi.

Belinda Norton and Abigail Carr
Montrose
Thursday 8:00 PM, Sept 7, 2000

Things were not turning out as Belinda had expected. Abigail Carr was not a typical author bored by reading her own book aloud numerous times on a book tour mandated by her publisher to increase sales. She had such passion and personal charisma that Belinda was irresistibly drawn to her. Not since her days of political rallies with Nikki Applegate had she felt so invigorated, so gloriously female.

When Laverne introduced Abigail to the couple standing near her, Belinda attempted to turn away in time to avoid meeting the author's eyes. Too late. Abigail looked her over slowly from head to foot and instantly made her decision. Though both women had very personalized agendas for the night ahead, a change was inevitable when their eyes met. Belinda's—intelligent, curious, and willing opened wide. Abigail's—aglow with vitality and a lust rarely visible in public places.

When the older woman finished reading, Belinda was standing nearby daring to catch her eye and draw her close enough for a private conversation. As they drifted away from the center of the room, the heat radiating from the two women left a smoky trail behind that felt as if a self-cleaning oven had been turned on without the timer being set.

Carla McCarthy and Nan Lawson
Montrose
Thursday evening Sept 7, 2000

I see an old acquaintance checking out the campaign posters plastered on the plate glass windows. The busy commercial area along the 9 Mile Rd. dining and shopping strip is Montrose's best place for the local candidates to campaign. Seventeen people are running for the six City Council and they all have signs, bumper stickers, and posters. My Sister's Books prominently displayed half a dozen colorful flyers for Fred Love, the openly gay candidate for City Council president.

"Matt Blanke, how are you? Still working at the Daily Snooz?" I don't see a cameraman tagging along with him so it is clear the paper does not consider Abigail Carr a big story.

He shrugs noncommittally. "Just here for the food and the wine, McCarthy. You know how reporters are," he said while he readjusted his bifocals to bring me into focus.

A few minutes later, I'm delighted when the current mayor shows up. "Looks like you forgot this is an election year."

"I knew I should have brought along a camera man." I can see Matt is disappointed he is going to miss these pictures.

I nod with feigned sympathy; "The race for Council seats is heating up this year. I think it might turn from the traditional low grade skirmish into an armed battle."

My camera is loaded and I have two extra rolls of film in my camera bag. I can't pass up a chance to have an exclusive of the portly Mayor Brooks. I take a few extra pictures to make sure I will have something good for tomorrow's paper. I don't plan to offer to share mine with Matt unless he asks. I don't think he will. That would mean he would owe me a favor that he might not be prepared to repay.

I point my camera around the room to see what else might be of interest. Although her publicist had provided me with a few standard headshots of Abigail, she looks so alluring; I can't resist taking several of my own photos of her. Any that the paper doesn't decide to run can go into my private scrapbook. A striking black woman is talking intently to her, dressed in dark brown silk from head to toe and wearing enough gold jewelry to make me wonder if Tiffany's had just been knocked off. She is obviously someone special. You don't get a look like that in five minutes. Oh, no, that woman has obviously been blown dry from head to toe, if you know what I mean. She is leaning forward to hear above the buzz of the crowd and doesn't see me taking pictures at first. When she notices the flash from my camera, she turns her face away and tries to fade into the crowd.

The phone is ringing again, so I stride over to the counter to see why no one is picking up. Just as I get there it stops ringing, and I take it off the hook. I am sure Laverne and Shirley will not want it ringing in the middle of Abby's book reading.

After the reading, Abby autographs at least three dozen books and everyone seems pleased with the results of the evening. I offer to take her back to her hotel, but to my dismay, she seems to have made other plans. Ginger still has not shown up or called, and I am beginning to be concerned about her. Something unexpected must have happened. She is the most dependable person I know, and if she is not here, something must be wrong.

By ten thirty, almost everyone has left. "Carla, are you ready to go?" Nan asks. "C'mon, let's walk out together. Don't tell me you left your precious five ton hunk of chrome in the alley?"

"Of course! Dinah is waiting faithfully for me," I chuckle as Nan and I walk out together. "I know I can always depend on her."

Some of my friends who think they are so clever call my car "Dinah," short for Dinosaur. My pink De Soto is alone at the rear of the empty lot. Abigail and I could have walked the short block to the bookstore from the café but I wanted to give her a ride in my vintage car. Apparently, neither my car nor I impressed her. The lot was crowded when we arrived, so I had to park facing the alley in the shadows, and I'm secretly relieved to have the police chief walk me to my car. Not that I am afraid. Montrose has a reputation as a safe neighborhood, but two's company and what better twosome than the Chief and me?

"It feels like rain," she comments quietly, as a humid little breeze rakes the littered parking lot.

"M-m-m-nice. I hope so, night time rain is my favorite," I say as I unlock the door and turn, hoping for a platonic hug.

Before I am able to turn all the way around, she leans in with both arms pressed against the car door with me right in the middle.

"My favorite too," she murmurs, sounding impossibly seductive, as she grasps my hands firmly and forces me back against the car.

Her lips press against mine, smooth and tight for a moment, and then without enough warning, our bodies relax and our lips release the tension and allow our breaths to touch. Before that permission reaches our tongues, she pulls away abruptly. "You must be practicing witchcraft tonight or I'm losing my mind."

"Neither, there's a full moon behind those clouds."

"Get into your car and go home before you get us into trouble." Her husky voice was almost back to normal.

Dinah is on remote control and gets us home safely while I daydream about the two new women in my life. Abigail is wildly exciting and worldly, and I feel like we had a special connection in the short time we had spent together. Nan, on the other hand, is sweet and unpredictable. Tonight was the second time she has kissed me in the twenty years we have been friends. Both times were unforgettable.

Skip is delirious to see me and wags his tail so hard he knocks a couple of oatmeal raisin cookies off the plate on the coffee table. I have him well trained, and he knows he can't go out until we have cleaned up all of the crumbs. While taking care of the cookies, I check my answering machine. Calls from a long distance telephone company and a neighborhood handy man can be ignored safely, but I am surprised by a message left by Maria just a few minutes before I arrived home.

"Carla? I'm sorry about tonight. I didn't mean to act like that. It's just that I lose my temper sometimes, you know? Darilyn is trying to steal my business and right now, I can't afford that. She is evil, and you'll find that out soon enough. Anyway, I just want you to know how sorry I am for everything. Please don't be mad. I really need to talk to you."

I wonder if Maria has been losing money at the casinos again. She has become friendly with some well to do women who gamble compulsively and I'm afraid she is not going to be able to keep up with them for long. Owning an Italian restaurant is not the same as being rich.

I hear a low rumble of far off thunder. Skip doesn't like thunder and lightening as much as I do, so we get in bed and cover our heads with the down comforter Ginger gave us for Christmas a couple years ago.

I am pleased that Nan was right with her prediction of rain.

Darilyn D'Angelo
Montrose
Thursday 9:00 PM, Sept. 7, 2000

Normally on Thursday nights, the vegetarian restaurant would be empty by 9:00, and Darilyn could leave if she had plans. Tonight, however, two customers lingered. It wasn't often that a man would come in for dinner alone, but tonight a man sat in a candlelit booth by himself and another, larger man sat at a table in the middle of the room where he could see both doors.

The younger man was inexpensively dressed in worn Dockers, and a blue button down shirt. He seemed distraught and looked at her resentfully when she asked if he would require anything else before the kitchen closed.

"You're not closing early tonight, are you?" He wiped perspiration from his brow, although the restaurant was cool. "The sign on the door says you are open till ten on Thursdays. I'm waiting for someone."

"If no one comes in after nine, I close up early during the week," she explained. "But there is no need for you to hurry. Enjoy your crème brulee."

The other man seemed lost in thought. He seemed to enjoy his dinner, but it was obvious to Darilyn that he did not care about the food. When she had taken his order earlier, he had not looked at the menu. "Just bring me whatever is good tonight, please." He gave her a big smile, but she hadn't felt it and he hadn't meant it.

When she noticed the man in the booth had blown out the candle on his table and was sitting huddled close to the wall, she felt a moment's unease. It was almost as if the man wanted to disappear into the gloom.

The big man at the table in the middle of the dining room kept looking at his watch as though he too was expecting someone to come in. Promptly at ten o'clock he walked to the cash register, paid his bill, and left. As Darilyn cleared his table, she was surprised to find a twenty-dollar bill next to his still full water glass.

As though his departure was a signal, the tall, dark haired man quickly finished his coffee and approached the cash register where she stood. Her customary question to departing guests "Was everything all right?" was withheld for this last customer tonight. She noticed his tight jaw and was afraid whatever he was holding back was something she didn't want to hear. She breathed a sigh of relief when he left without incident.

When both men had gone, she locked the front door and extinguished all of the candles in the front dining room. For a few minutes, Darilyn busied herself checking for vases that would need fresh flowers tomorrow and straightening the tablecloths. The empty restaurant felt different tonight. Maybe she should take everyone's advice and have someone stay with her until closing time during the week.

Belinda should have been here by now. She was usually early. It was one of her most endearing qualities, how eager she was to spend time with Darilyn. China Jane was expecting them at her place no later than ten thirty. Darilyn was hoping Jane had persuaded Ginger to join them.

Impulsively grabbing her sweater and keys from her small office, Darilyn hastily left a note for Belinda to wait for her. She would walk to Jane's in two or three minutes to make sure Belinda was not waiting for her there. The narrow sidewalk provided a space for customers to walk from store to store without ever going around to 9 Mile. The businesses along the strip all had rear entrances for the convenience of their customers who parked in the public lot.

The moonless night air was cool and felt like rain as she crossed 9 Mile Rd. and slipped unobtrusively through Jane's unlocked rear door. For a brief moment, she worried about leaving her door unlocked, but she had promised Belinda she would, and besides, she would be right back. Jane's back door opened onto a small hallway with another door that led to the basement.

The door creaked as she opened it, and when she fumbled for the light switch, it clicked, but the lights on the stairs stayed off. "Jane? It's me. Anybody here?" She could hear music from Jane's little radio coming from the lower level. She cautiously took each step down the unlit stairwell with one hand feeling the way down along the clammy cement wall. The steep stairs made her uneasy. They were too familiar in her frequent dreams of falling.

"We're in the back, come on in," Jane replied from the back room. Darilyn wished the women would agree to meet at her place more often. It was much nicer, but Tootsie liked to stay in her own building and Jane usually went along with her.

After an uncomfortable few minutes of heated conversation it was decided that Jane would walk back over to Vegelina's to look for the errant Belinda.

As soon as Jane left, Darilyn looked around for a bathroom. She wanted to avoid a conversation with Tootsie, who looked as if she was going to cry. There was a unisex upstairs that Jane always kept clean so she ventured back up the dark stairs again.

She heard someone come in just before she flushed and she was relieved that Jane was back so quickly. She must have found Belinda in the parking lot. Her feeling of relief when she exited the bathroom and reached the top stair was snatched away by a scene from a horror movie. The same tall good looking man who had been in her restaurant earlier stepped out of the shadows in the corner and forcefully grabbed her arm with one hand and quickly clapped his other hand over her mouth before she could scream for help.

Title IX

Athletic competition builds character in our boys. We do not need that kind of character in our girls.
Connecticut judge, 1971

No person in the United States shall, on the basis of sex, be excluded from participation in, be denied the benefits of, or be subject to discrimination under any educational programs or activity receiving federal financial assistance.
From the preamble to Title IX of the Education Amendments of 1972 Civil rights

Barbara Jane and RJ Brown
Detroit
Summer 1956

RJ suddenly grew four inches when I was eleven and he was nine. No one in my family expected that he would ever catch up to me. He was bigger than most of the kids in his class; sometimes people thought we were twins. Dad put up a basketball hoop on the garage for us. I knew it was meant for RJ but he always let me play too. As soon as RJ was old enough for middle school, Dad signed him up for Little League basketball. When I asked why I couldn't play, RJ's coach told Dad, "We don't have a girl's baseball or basketball team because girls don't play those sports." During school breaks and summer vacations RJ would play softball and even football with me, but at school, I could only play girl sports—volleyball and swimming.

I never got over feeling that it was not fair I was not allowed to play.

❦   ❦   ❦

RJ wanted to be a baseball player for the New York Yankees when he grew up. He never changed his mind. He was like that. He never changed his mind about anything. We all thought he would forget about being RJ and go back to being Bobby, but he never did. Mama said he wasn't stubborn, he just knew what he wanted. He took after our father's side of the family. You could always depend on RJ.

Mimi wanted to be a singer for a while after we heard Kate Smith sing "God Bless America" on the Ed Sullivan show. Later, when her Aunt Irene started taking her to Saturday matinees, she wanted to be a movie star like Marilyn Monroe or maybe Elizabeth Taylor. When she got a little older, she started making plans to be either a rabbi or a housewife. Mama told us "Mimi is just plumb capricious. Maybe she should prepare to go wherever the road takes her."

It was harder for me to say what I was going to be when I grew up. After a lot of thought, Mama said, "Barbara Jane, you can be what ever you want to be, so whatever you pick, you better make sure you are ready for it."

My first career was preordained by the time I was ten and in the fifth grade at Beaubien Middle School. I just didn't realize it until much later. My life in those days was filled with calming tiny chipmunks that were in shock after the neighbor's dog noisily pursued them until they found refuge under our back porch. When curiosity drove our cat to investigate the chirping noises coming from a temporarily unguarded nest in the crabapple tree, I comforted three slightly comatose baby jays. I even persuaded RJ to collect some worms for me so I could feed the baby birds that had fallen out of the nest. Frogs and toads occasionally found their way to my examining room just because they looked so strange.

"Old Maid" Patrick changed my life in the sixth grade when we had Career Day. Our school nurse wore thick glasses and was not married although my Mother said she was at least thirty-five. During an outbreak of the flu, my homeroom teacher arranged her visit to our classroom to give us a hygiene lesson. When Miss Patrick asked for a volunteer, I hopefully raised my hand. When she picked me, I smugly went to the front of the class.

Miss Patrick held my hands in the basin of warm water and carefully lathered each finger one by one. It tickled when she spread the creamy soap into the palms and onto the backs of my hands. When her hands circled my wrists, it was the most wonderful feeling. I was smitten with the smell of Ivory soap mingled with Jungle Gardenia, and I forgot I was in the front of the classroom with everyone looking at me. When she couldn't find a speck of dirt anywhere on my hands, she took a worn terry cloth towel and dried each finger. Finished, she held up my clean hands for everyone's approval. I gave a victorious smile to the entire class, and any uncertainty I may have had evaporated. I knew that day I wanted to be a nurse.

I wonder if Miss Patrick ever knew she held my fate in her hands that day.

Carla McCarthy
Montrose
Friday 9:00 AM, September 8, 2000

"Thank God it's Friday, thank God it's Friday," is my repeated chant to myself as I try to decide if I should park in the back of the Candid Times lot and avoid any potential dings to my darling De Soto, or if I should park close to the door and keep my new Louis Vuitton shoes out of the puddles.

An early morning thunderstorm rattling and howling through town just before dawn caused me to stay snuggled safely in bed long after the alarm buzzed. A pleasant cloud surrounded me as though I had been having a wonderful dream. When I was awake enough to remember the kiss in the parking lot was not a dream, I snuggled deeper into my pillow for a moment of secret smiles.

Trying to avoiding rush hour traffic is an admirable goal even when the weather is good, which in Michigan is about two weeks a year. Detroit and its suburbs will never have mass transit. To remain the automotive capital of the world they figure they need 2.5 automobiles for every man, woman and child on the roads at all times. The drive from Montrose to Royal Oak was the worst in the history of the world, and now the parking lot is full of puddles as big as Grosse Pointe swimming pools. It doesn't seem fair that my parking choices are limited by the dozen or so Times hourly employees who pride themselves on making it to work on time and took all o f the good spots.

Pulling into the last row, I reach into the back seat for my emergency Princess Bag and pull out my Totes. Pete will razz me when he sees me sloshing through the office in my rubber boots, but his usual Casual Friday attire includes run down loafers from Payless Shoe Store along with twill Dockers that have seen better days. Not that I am a shoe snob. Other people are perfectly free to wear whatever kind of footwear they want, but my footwear will not get wet if I can possibly help it.

Mr. Millbourne started publishing The Candid Times as a weekly newspaper sometime in the seventies. Charley Millbourne worked at the New York Times for many years before semi-retiring in Montrose to be close to his wife's family. The first edition he published had the Candid Times Ethics Standards printed on the front page. That impressed readers who had never seen such a thing and probably didn't know it existed. Subscriptions grew every year as Montrose and the surrounding suburbs grew. Readers liked Millbourne's philosophy of treating them fairly and honestly. Under the banner was a statement he borrowed from the NY Times: "The Times gathers information for the benefit of its readers."

Pete planned to earn his way through college working here. He started part time as a copy boy, but after he was kicked out of Wayne State for stealing a teacher's lesson plans and selling them, he started working full time at anything Mr. M needed him to do. When Mr. Millbourne's mother-in-law died, his wife insisted they were ready to retire and move to Florida, and he let Pete buy the Times at a fair price.

I asked Pete one time how he could afford to buy the Times. Without the windfall from my book, I would have been paying off my college loans until I was forty. He reluctantly told me his Mother loaned him her retirement savings to help him finance the start-up and his family co-signed his loans at the credit union. He would be making payments to the bank for thirty years. Pete's beginner's luck was good, and the paper burgeoned into a successful daily evening paper when the Detroit dailies went on strike in the early nineties. Subscriptions were on the rise and the Times was on its way to becoming a viable family resource for national news as well as the best local entertainment source in the tri-county area.

As fast as Pete made money in the early days, he invested it right back into the paper. He never spent any money on himself, but the paper had to have the best equipment money could buy. When he moved into a larger building, he went into debt and bought a more efficient printing press, installed air conditioning, and built a bigger parking lot for the employees. His need for the biggest and best of everything made me apprehensive. I was raised in a home where debt was looked upon as a modern day evil. My Irish Dad constantly preached to us kids, "If you can't pay cash for it, don't buy it."

With the Detroit Free Press and the Detroit News back in business now, the Times is on the verge of becoming just a weekly tabloid again. The bills are not being paid, and Pete is under a lot of financial pressure to make timely mortgage payments. If he defaults, Mr. M can take the paper back. If something doesn't change, Pete will never be able to pay his mother back. The whole community was shocked six months ago when, without any fanfare, the Times started running Wild Hearts ads for the so-called Alternative Lifestyle readers. It wasn't the first time Pete shocked his regular readers. Two years ago when he was taking money out of his own pocket to make the payroll, he started running Lonely Hearts notices and even accepting sleazy 900 number ads. The public indignation about that blew over eventually, and I figure it will over this too.

A couple of years ago, when we still had interns from the Journalism department at Wayne working here, he accidentally discovered I have "lesbian tendencies." At the time, I had been on the verge of quitting more than once. I was outraged to learn Pete had copies of the keys to my office and had been reading my personal notes that I kept locked in my desk. I cleaned the trumpery off my desk and was on my way out the door when I thought about my three animals at home that depend on me. Pete considers himself a liberal, but every once in a while his puritanical upbringing comes through. We don't talk about it, which makes it easier for both of us. When he is in a bad mood, he can be quite nasty, and it's uncomfortable being on the receiving end of his sarcasm.

An even bigger financial responsibility is my ex and our berry farm. Although Kerry and I separated several years ago, we still share the farm on the western side of the state. When I need to get away, especially in August when the raspberries and blackberries are ripe, I go spend a few days there. When members of my book club and Mensa groups talk about their real estate investments and the stock market, I just keep my mouth shut. You can't beat blueberries for security. Lately, blueberry farmers are doing better than the Big Three automobile companies are. Michigan grows a third of all the blueberries eaten in the US. No need for imported berries in the Michigan, we grow over fifty million pounds a year here. My Mom makes blueberry pies, blueberry muffins, blueberry ice cream, blueberry buckle, and even puts blueberries in salads with the berries I bring home. Kerry does most of the work and during the summer, she hires the neighbors' kids to help her with the mixed berry preserves she sells to specialty markets. We both thought for a while I would come back someday but now it looks like that is not going to happen.

Pete's Mother is the one I can't figure out. Pete has talked to me about her ever since I started at the paper. When things were good, she worked from home and took care of the payroll and the books. When Pete laid off the two part time interns, Mrs. Brown started coming in every day and took over answering the telephone and taking the Personal Ads. She insists on sitting by herself in a very small office that is actually the space where the phone equipment is located. She seems devoted to Pete, but there is a streak of aloofness or maybe grandiosity in her that just doesn't seem to fit. I've never seen her wear make-up or jewelry, and she must buy her Dr Scholl's knock-offs at the same Payless Shoe Store Pete shops at.

New employees, when they find out she is Pete's Mother, try to make friends with her, but she prefers to eat lunch alone in her office with the door closed. She avoids me too, but I don't take it personally.

I asked Pete one time why she doesn't seem to like anyone and all he would say was, "Ah, you know. My Dad died in Vietnam and she's had it hard. She had a beauty shop for awhile but things didn't work out. She's lonely. I'm all she has now. My aunt just moved back to Michigan. Maybe she will be company for her."

I dropped it then. Sometimes my big family drives me crazy, but I can't imagine not having brothers and sisters and aunts and uncles and cousins. When my aunt's husband died, she came to live with us. There was always room for one more at our house. Two legged or four legged, it didn't matter.

Pete and I have always had a difference of opinion on how to run the paper. He feels inferior because he didn't finish college, and I know my Master's degree in Journalism intimidates him but that is no excuse for his stubbornness. A few months after he bought the paper, he removed Mr. M's motto from the banner.

When the motto went, the ethics code was close behind. I tried to explain to Pete that there is a certain creed in journalism that is at the heart of the newspaper business, but he just didn't get it. To him, being the owner of a newspaper meant he could sell ads.

"Didn't you ever work on your high school paper?"

His answer summed up his lack of experience. "Hell, no. I was too busy delivering papers and washing cars after school to write for a newspaper. I didn't come from a rich family."

My real paycheck comes from my Astrology Columns that the dailies have picked up. I started writing them as a lark a few years ago when some other laid off friends and I were killing time at the New Moon Coffee Shop. I read the Candid Times Aries horoscope aloud to the group one afternoon and everyone yawned and groaned. To impress an attractive woman sitting with us, I made up a much more interesting horoscope for Leos and then everyone wanted to hear theirs. As they shouted out their signs, I made up something for each of them.

Celebrate, Lovely Leo. You will soon find yourself awash in Brummagems. Someone has mistaken you for a BlingAholic. Buy yourself one special piece of jewelry this week and see what happens. While you are at it, buy something for that person you have been ogling from a safe distance. It is easier to catch a big fish when you are willing to bait the hook. All that glitters is worth checking out at least once.

Salud, Scorpio. Set your free spirit free. In other words, don't sweat the small stuff! When you find yourself running late for an appointment, Rejoice! A very special encounter that will change your life is near. If you want to meet a Star, you must not forego your morning Starbucks ritual just because you overslept. If you aspire to be a Star, your mornings should be spent in pursuit of a different form of stimulus.

Awake, Aries. Your affirmation for today is: The difference between safe and SaME is ME. You can eat corn flakes every morning and be safe but you will never hear a snap or feel a crunch. Live your life for just one day where nothing you do or say is the same as you have done every other day of your corn flake life. When you wake up, drink a Curacao martini. If it is a workday, dress in blue velvet. Buy primroses and give them to a stranger for no reason. Eat blueberry muffins on the beach for dinner. The next time you want to turn in early go to a funky bar and listen to the Blues. There now, doesn't that feel better?

<u>Relax, Gemini</u>. For some people the rule is, *If you want something done right, you must do it yourself.* Don't listen to that nonsense! Your role during this lifetime is to lead. Occasionally that may mean to lead by example, but with the stars bright in the sky this month your role is to create action by inspiration, not perspiration. If you can conceive it, someone else can deliver it. When the doorbell rings, throw open the door with great anticipation…the delivery in a plain brown wrapper is for you!

<u>Toot! Toot! Taurus</u>. It's not a secret why they named a car after you—You're sleek and shiny and you love to go places. One caution for you, dear. Don't forget there is a brake pedal as well as a gas pedal. You tend to abandon caution, especially when skilled hands are on the wheel. Your loyalty is to be commended but keep in mind you that will have many drivers before your life is over and they all will deserve your concern if not your love. Keep your headlights on in dark spaces and you'll be fine. Bon Voyage!

I found I had a natural knack for coming up with unique forecasts, and a career was born. My monthly syndication check pays the rent, and whatever I can freelance supports my immodest shoe habit.

I'm eager to see Pete's banged-up Saturn pull into the parking lot. The pictures I took of the Mayor hobnobbing with an eclectic group at the bookstore last night should make the front page. There were more than a handful of homosexuals there, and I saw two witches checking out the greeting card section. I have plenty of time to make the weekend edition with a one thousand-word article about the City Council election and the candidates.

With the Carr interview, I will have two spots with my by-line on them and if I hurry, maybe I can get the restaurant review done too. Pete likes to brag that he gets free meals based on the restaurant reviews I write. I don't know how many restaurant owners actually know who I am, but of course, I always pay for my meals, and I use a pseudonym on all of my printed reviews to avoid any signs of favoritism. Just one more small area where he and I disagree on the right thing to do.

When my cell rings a little after nine, Pete has not come in yet. It's Frankie. I've never heard her cry before.

"Ginger still has not come home!"

Summer passes and one remembers one's exuberance.

—Yoko Ono

Barbara Jane
Detroit
Summer 1956

Summers seemed so special in those days. Mom let me sleep in late and stay up late too. Some magical moment only my Mother recognized signaled the official start of summer to our family. It was somewhere between May Day and Decoration Day. Screens were brought out of the basement and replaced the heavy storm windows. The windows were washed, and I would wake up in my upstairs bedroom hearing the chickadees and cardinals singing in the trees outside my window. The fragrance of apple blossoms and fresh new grass came through the opened windows on the vernal breezes.

Summer days were magically imbued with seemingly endless possibilities.

On Tuesdays, Mom would drive RJ and me to Palmer Park where we could swim all morning in the new pool. Mimi usually agreed to come with us. After a picnic lunch, Mother allowed us to run off to explore the fountains or the wooden cabin Mr. Palmer had built for his wife a long time ago.

Even on rainy days, we found ways to have fun in the house. Mom would make strawberry Jell-O with tiny banana slices and give us the empty boxes to cut up. If we cut out the J.E.L.L.O. letters carefully enough, we could glue them together to make a Jell-O man or woman. In the afternoons when RJ was at practice and Mom was lying down reading one of her True Story magazines, Mimi and I would get the spare blankets out of the linen cupboard, push the dining room chairs together, and make a tent where we would whisper and giggle until Dad came home.

"Barbara Jane, where are you? Is Mimi here? Oh dear, I hope those young-uns have not run away with the circus," Dad would tease.

Some days, I would take the blue Pendleton blanket from my room into our backyard, lie as far away from the garbage-burning pit as I could get, and read Nancy Drew mysteries from the library. When I tired of reading, I would turn over, look up at the clouds, and imagine the future. Other days I would bounce a rubber ball off the front steps and catch it with my brother's leather mitt for mindless hours until my Mother made me come in for dinner.

Mama saved empty mayonnaise jars and washed them for us to use, and Dad would poke nail holes in the lids. At dusk, we took the jars outside to catch fireflies. After I had caught a couple of the nocturnal beetles, I didn't want to do it any more. I suddenly realized they actually might be fairies like Tinker Bell. I convinced Mimi and RJ to let the ones they caught go free too. From then on, we were content to watch the fireflies' dance in that magic twilight hour which belonged to them. For a few weeks every July and August, fireflies and their invisible consorts, the mischievous leprechauns, were the subjects of our favorite bedtime stories.

After the firefly amnesty went into effect, Dad took RJ out on forays into the damp grass in front of the house just after dark. He wanted to teach RJ to find nightcrawlers using only a big flashlight. Dad had rarely gone fishing since we moved to Michigan, but he wanted RJ to know the right way to find his own bait.

He said it was okay if I wanted to talk to the fairies, but he wanted RJ to be all boy.

Carla McCarthy
Montrose
Friday Morning, Sept 8, 2000

Frankie is bombarding me with questions so fast I can't grasp the real problem. "Do you think she has been kidnapped? Has she called you? She's not with you, is she? I have been driving around all night looking for her. Her car is still in the Nine Mile Rd. lot."

I don't want to get in the middle of this but my first words when she takes a breath are, "I can't believe Ginger would be so irresponsible to leave her car in that lot all night." I'm immediately ashamed of myself. Just because my car is so important to me, I'm sure Frankie couldn't care less about Ginger's damn car right now.

That comment doesn't help calm her down, but I can't think of anything to say that will make it all right. It would be so out of character for Ginger to be out all night with another woman. Something must have happened to her. Either way, Frankie is going to go ballistic. I know I can't let her know how worried I am too.

I only can get her off the phone with a promise to check out some things and put in a call to Chief Lawson's private number.

❧   ❧   ❧

When Nan answers, I hear the tension in her voice, and I wonder if she already knows something about Ginger. I start to tell her and she abruptly cuts me off with the terse statement, "There's been a murder at Vegelina's and Darilyn D'Angelo is missing." She hears my gasp and pauses while I blurt out, "So is Ginger."

"Oh shit," Nan exhaled audibly.

"Any chance they are together? You know, maybe they rented a U-haul?" Another wildly inappropriate joke on my part before it sinks in that Nan said there had been a murder.

"Don't joke, Carla," Nan warns. "One woman is already dead and now two more are missing."

She quickly fills me in before asking more about Ginger.

Guardian Alarm called the Montrose police department last night a little after twelve when no one from Vegelina's had called to set the alarm at closing time. Sometimes there was a late customer, but when the alarm company called to check, no one answered the telephone. A patrol car drove by sometime between one and six AM but didn't see anything out of the ordinary.

When Nan started her shift at seven this morning, she sent a two-man patrol car to check out the complaint more thoroughly. Within minutes, Lt. Joe Riley called in for homicide back up, an EMT unit, and the Medical Examiner.

Riley's preliminary report stated he found the heavy back door closed but not locked. Upon announcing himself and receiving no answer, he entered the building and found a woman's nude body sprawled in the center of the kitchen lying in a small pool of dark blood.

"It's not Darilyn? Oh, no! Could it be Ginger?" I asked with some trepidation. "Who is it Nan?"

"Carla, I can't tell you anything yet," Nan answered flatly.

Barbara Jane and Mimi
Detroit
Autumn 1959

Mimi and I were inseparable during my early teenage years. We walked to school together, and when I went to Mumford and made new friends, I still hurried home to tell her about my day and my classes. She seemed older than RJ, and we confided things to each other that no one else knew. When I told her I was in love with Bridgett Bardot, she told me I would have to take French lessons if I wanted to talk to her. We were at an age where the idea of taking French lessons brought about gales of laughter. French kissing was something the kids in our neighborhood talked about but didn't really understand. Patty Clark had the advantage of an older brother she spied on when his girlfriend came to their house to study. She demonstrated for us up in my room one afternoon. "Ooh! You've got cooties now," was our initial reaction to her putting her tongue in our mouths.

When Patty went home for dinner, we were curious enough to try it again. That was the year we later called The Bardot Year. Mimi said we had to practice so when she and RJ got married, she would be the best kisser in Detroit.

Things heated up when Mimi nonchalantly asked me if she could borrow my training bra. "Let me see," I demanded. Even though I was two years older, I still was almost flat, but suddenly Mimi started to have soft curved breasts. She was the envy of all of the girls in her class and even some of the girls in my class. Patty told me that people were saying Mimi must have been letting some boy touch her tits, that is why they were so big. The other theory, which was even worse, was that maybe Mimi was "doing it." I knew from personal experience that just touching your breasts wouldn't make them big.

We were both curious why her breasts were growing and mine weren't. Hers were soft and plump and mine were flat with small, hard nipples. It wasn't hard to convince Mimi to let me frequently examine her. She knew I was going to be a nurse.

Neither Mimi nor I dated in middle school. She was waiting for RJ and I was just waiting.

Carla McCarthy
Montrose
10:00 AM, Friday, Sept 8, 2000

Pete and his Mother pulled into the parking lot a little before ten. I can hear the worn brakes screech, which means Pete was driving too fast again. He looks surprised to see me sitting at his desk. Looking apprehensively around the room, he asks, "Something wrong McCarthy, or are you just indulging your fantasy of being the boss?"

"There was a woman murdered in Montrose last night" I reply tersely. "And two other women are missing," I add standing up. Coming out from behind his desk, I fill him in on what little I know about the murdered woman and the restaurant where she was found. "The Montrose police found a woman's body in Vegelina's on 9 Mile Road this morning about eight o'clock."

"Isn't that where you were interviewing the author last night? Do you know the woman who owns the place?"

"I know her Pete, her name is Darilyn D'Angelo, but that is not who was killed. Chief Lawson said she is missing and someone else was found dead in her restaurant."

He looks shocked and I wonder if he could actually be worried about me being there the same night it happened.

I give him all of my notes about the murder and the restaurant, but I still hesitate to go with the missing women story so soon. I can't accept the possibility that Ginger is in any real danger.

"The Montrose PD will probably release the name of the victim and approximate time of death before noon today." Taking another sip of coffee, I suggest, "Let's get a stand-alone story ready to go to press about the murder. We can add the missing women angle if they don't turn up soon."

Pete reluctantly agrees we should get a special edition out right away since we seem to have the inside track for the moment. I want to be cautious in case it turns out that Ginger is only having a fling. I know anything I say this morning will be blown out of all proportion because the police are investigating a homicide. It's probably only a coincidence that Ginger went on an unplanned sleepover.

"This is a big story Carla. I'll need you to follow up on the murdered woman right away. Can we can postpone filing the social events from last night?" Pete asks me more or less rhetorically as he commandeers his chair and desk.

"Of course, Pete, but I've got some great candids of the mayor on this roll of film as well as the author from last night."

"Okay. Great job, McCarthy." He is already dismissing me.

"Will you have the lab develop the film right away?"

"Sure, sure, I'll tell 'em you get the photo credit for any thing we can use. Be sure you call me first if you find out anything. Anything at all, I want to know first. Understand?"

I would rather have more cash than the photo credit, but that is not going to happen. Pete Brown might be the only person I know with less actual cash than me. At least I don't owe my mother money. His desk is a mess as always with newspaper clippings, two soggy half-full paper coffee cups, what looks like yesterday's lunch, and a stack of unopened bills. I put the roll of film in an envelope on his chair and write THE MAYOR in Magic Marker so he won't miss it.

❧   ❧   ❧

Vegelina's is my first stop when I leave the Times. It has stopped raining, but the cement sidewalk still has that clean, just washed look. From the front, the place looks vacant, but when I pull into the lot behind the building, crime scene yellow barricade tape is stretched across the rear entrance.

An official looking black Ford panel van has backed up to the building. Two evidence technicians are working just inside the restaurant's propped open back door. "Got a report yet?"

Shaking her head, the taller one replies, "No way, McCarthy. You know it will be a couple of days before we have anything official."

"Well, can you at least give me an ID?" I lower my voice and edge closer to the tape in case I get lucky and she actually tells me something.

"Female, about thirty. Looks as though she may have been on a date, fresh manicure, expensive jewelry. Anything else they will have to give you at the station."

"Thanks, I owe you one. Marge, right?"

"Close, it's Margo," she replied with a forgiving grin. "You can buy me a beer next time I see you at the Girl's."

❦   ❦   ❦

It is a fifteen-minute drive to Frankie's house in Palmer Park. I have to break the news about the murder to Frankie in person. Her red pick up truck is parked in the drive. The rain didn't do it's job here last night. The big truck still needs a wash; the rain has just made it look dirtier.

She is watching out the front window and opens the door as I'm coming up the steps. "What's wrong, Carla? What's happened?"

I can feel her fear, and waiting won't make it go away.

"The police found a dead woman in Vegelina's early this morning."

I wait for the reaction I know is coming. She looks blank for about ten seconds before her face starts to crumble. "Ah man, that's terrible. It's nobody we know, right?"

Frankie disappears into the kitchen to get us a beer. She doesn't want me to see her crying. I keep looking out the window at her pick-up in the driveway. I know if I see her crying, I will be crying too. Ginger would not stay out all night without leaving someone a message. If she is going to be even a few minutes late anywhere, she always calls. Something is seriously wrong. Dead wrong.

Now there is a body to confirm that opinion.

"Uh, Frankie? How do you feel about praying?" I ask with some hesitation. "I think we should pray that Ginger is okay."

Frankie belongs to the Mt. Olive Baptist church although she doesn't go very often, anymore. She took me there once so I could hear authentic, gospel music.

"Yeah, sure, Carla, if you think so," Frankie nods. "You and Ginger are best friends. You're my best friend too. Man, I couldn't get through this without you." Frankie keeps running her fingers through her short tightly curled hair, and I just want to grab her hand and hold it, to keep it from shaking.

Holding a cold bottle of Heineken in one hand and clutching Frankie's hand with the other, I say The Unity Prayer for Protection. It's the only one I can remember so I use it for everything, and so far, in my life it has worked pretty well.

"Dear God,
Let your light shine down upon us,
Let your love enfold us,
Let your power protect us, (and Ginger, too)
Let your presence surround us,
And we know wherever we are,
You are and all is well.
Dear God, please let Ginger be safe and come home soon.
Thank you and Amen"

I help Frankie go through an old address book Ginger left there. It takes us more than an hour to call everyone in there. Frankie even insists on calling Ginger's dentist and hairdresser. Some of the area codes are old ones going back several years before the phone company changed all of the suburban Detroit numbers from 313 to 248 and 586.

I try to reach Nan, but her private line is routing to her assistant today. Mike did give me the name of the victim but he didn't have any more he could tell me. I call Pete next and explain I am busy tracking down the two missing women, one of whom is a very good friend of mine. He knows Ginger slightly, she has come by the office to meet me for lunch a few times, and she asked him once to donate space for a weekly Adopt-A-Pet feature for MACS. He turned her down rather abruptly and there have been hard feelings on both sides since.

Of the handful of people Frankie and I can reach, no one has seen or heard from Ginger. "Frankie, we have to call the police now," I say slowly. "It's up to you to officially report her missing. I told Nan this morning, but I know she is busy working on the murder at Vegelina's."

The officer who answers the phone takes the information reluctantly and informs Frankie that an adult is not considered missing until it has been 24 hours or foul play is suspected.

Of course, he has to ask the inevitable question that every gay couple dreads, especially inter-racial couples, "What is your relationship to the missing woman?"

Frankie brusquely tells him, "She is my best friend and it has been twenty-four hours since any one has seen her. Ginger would never leave her car in a parking lot over night and it is parked just one block from where the murder happened in Montrose last night."

That gets his attention, and after asking a few more questions, he opens a missing person case.

Rush hour traffic takes us back again to Montrose. I'm glad to see Ginger's car is still parked in the lot behind China Jane's restaurant. There is no sign of Jane in the kitchen windows when we pass by but I see Hannah, the one cook Jane can depend on. The place is not big but there is usually an available seat at lunchtime. The big crowds are here on the weekends with the never-ending take-out orders.

The only thing Chinese about Jane is the egg rolls and fried rice she sells. In fact, she is taller than average and her short hair is still mostly blond mixed with a lot of gray. She moves like a woman who has been playing ball for a long time, and her posture tells you she has either had years of martial arts training or ballet lessons. Jane frequently hires a cook to help in the kitchen, but she tells anyone who dares ask that all of the recipes are her own. There is one small sepia toned photo of Jane with several Asian people that Jane calls her family pinned up on the wall near the cash register. The picture is not a professional photo and looks as though it were taken a long time ago. She is probably taking a rare night off.

❧   ❧   ❧

"You got keys, Frankie?"

She nods. "Yeah, I have a spare set for both the car and to her house." Frankie is checking the glove box and trunk in Ginger's car for clues.

"Why don't you move it before the cops tow it? You could drive the car to Ginger's house and park it in the garage so it will be there when Ginger comes home."

"I don't know, Carla. It doesn't seem right for me to take her car. What if she comes back here looking for it?"

"Frankie, one of us has to go over there and let Buster and Scotty out. We can't just leave them alone locked up in the house. Ginger would never forgive us. The dogs are used to you. Go now, and I'll come over in a little while to pick you up if you don't want to stay there over night."

When my cell phone rings, I am happy to see it is Nan returning the numerous calls and messages I have left for her today.

"Carla, hi. Have you or Frankie heard anything from Ginger today?"

"Nan, have you found Darilyn? What is going on with the police investigation at Vegelina's?" I want to know everything, but I don't know what to ask first.

"Carla, what about Ginger?" Nan asks again, this time a little more sternly.

"No, neither of us has heard from Ginger," I remember to tell her. When the reporter in me meets the cop in her, she always wins.

I am surprised when Nan wants to meet both of us for dinner. The three of us quickly agree to meet at the Italian Gardens. It is noisy enough there that we can talk without being over heard and I can get a beer. Frankie is going to Ginger's house first to take care of the dogs and then she will meet us in an hour. I haven't had a plate of Maria's specialty, Eggplant Rollatini, in way too long, and I want to see Nan.

Mimi and RJ
Detroit
1963–1966

When Mimi and RJ were in the ninth grade, they started walking home from school together. I was the only one who one noticed. She had forgotten all about me, and so had RJ. My mother kept telling me it was only temporary, and I was too old for them anyway. I tried not to care. I invited Patty Clark over after school most afternoons, and we listened to Connie Francis and Brenda Lee in my room while we did our algebra homework. We were on the swim team together, and I said she was my best friend, but we both knew it was by default.

When RJ was at football practice, Mimi would join us. Since they had started going steady, all she talked about was herself and RJ. He gave her his school ring, which she wore around her neck on a chain. At our house, she wore the ring outside of her sweater, but I noticed she tucked it in when she went home. Her mother and father expected her to only date Jewish boys, but the only boy she had ever been interested in was RJ.

It was time for me to grow up and have my own friends. I graduated from Mumford in June of 1963. Our class song was "Our Day Will Come," and I honestly believed it. Patty's older brother took me to the prom, and that was the end of my unremarkable high school days.

Our day will come
And we'll have everything.
We'll share the joy
Falling in love can bring.
No one can tell me
That I'm too young to know (young to know)
I love you so (love you so)
And you love me.
Our day will come
If we just wait a while.
No tears for us—
Think love and wear a smile.
Our dreams have magic

Because we'll always stay
In love this way
Our day will come.
Our day will come

Patty and I both started nursing school at Wayne State the next semester. Mom and Dad said I could take the summer off and just have fun before I started school again, but I was ready to find out what being grown up was all about. I figured I had to make my own money to do that.

By the time they reached 12th grade RJ and Mimi's study nights and weekend movies had evolved into serious dating. If Miriam and Ira were disappointed that she had not found a nice Jewish boy, they were happy it was RJ. Since he was 12, he had cut their grass when Ira worked long hours in the store, he had helped Mrs. S carry in groceries, and our families celebrated together when RJ was valedictorian of their sophomore class.

The whole family was shocked when Dad let RJ use his Corvette to take Mimi to the prom that year. Her long waited for wish came true that night.

None of my wishes were coming true.

Carla and Nan Lawson
Montrose
Friday Evening, Sept 8, 2000

Maria looks startled when Nan and I walk in at the same time and sit down together. I wonder if her radar is working and we look like a couple. Maria knows me so well. We are early enough to get a good table without a reservation. Nan and I share an excellent house antipasto salad while we wait for Frankie, and she asks a few questions about Ginger. "Is she in debt? Are there any relationship problems I should know about? Has she been using drugs or drinking more than usual?" I'm feeling uncomfortable discussing Ginger like this, but there haven't been any big changes in her life in a long time that I am aware of. Ginger doesn't have an enemy in the world. No one would want to hurt her. Her family has a lot of old money but most people don't realize Ginger is from *the* Harris family of Harris Paper Company. Her Lexus is her only obvious indulgence and if anyone asks, Ginger tells them she got a good deal on a lease.

When I spot Frankie at the door looking around the room for us, it hits me how much older she looks tonight. She still has that blank, lost look on her face. I wave her over and hand her a menu when she sits down. She is not saying much to either Nan or me. I try to reassure her that Ginger is probably fine, just off on a little adventure. She looks at me as if I were insane.

When Nan abruptly starts to ask Frankie the same questions she asked me about Ginger, Frankie's eyes have the same scared look I've seen in murder suspects in a line-up. I feel like a voyeur and suddenly realize that Frankie may have something she doesn't want to say in front of me. After a few minutes, I leave the table and sit at the far end of the bar with Maria to give the two women some privacy.

Maria is ringing the cash register at her usual Friday night post. She is a great hostess, chatting with guests while they wait for their tables, answering the phone, taking last minute week-end reservations. The tremendous success of the Italian Gardens is not only because of Maria's famous Italian specialties but also because of Maria's hard work night after night.

"My staff is scared to death," Maria lowers her voice and tells me confidentially. "The police were here as soon as we opened today asking about Darilyn."

When I take a close look at my old friend, I realize she is not drinking tonight. She has on more make-up than usual, but she looks so tired. Her blue eyes, usually so clear, are bloodshot tonight. It could be she is just tired and hung over, but it looks as if she has been crying. Too late, I remember I didn't return her call from last night.

"Why are you here with the chief tonight? Does Frankie know the murdered woman?" Maria asks uneasily. "Or was this a date that got interrupted when Frankie showed up?"

"No, all I know about her is her name. It is definitely no one I have ever heard of before. Frankie and I were planning to have dinner here and Nan decided to join us at the last minute." I can't believe Maria would even consider pulling her jealous routine because I am having dinner with Nan Lawson.

I ask her, "How well do you know Darilyn? You seemed pretty annoyed with her last night. Do you two have some kind of feud going on?"

"She's a competitor; I'm not supposed to like her." Maria tries her familiar bratty smile but it doesn't work as well as usual tonight.

"You left me a message last night and you said I would find out she is evil. What did you mean by that? Did you know something about the murder when you called me?"

"Of course I didn't know about the murder! I just called to apologize. We've been friends a long time. I just wanted to make sure you weren't mad at me."

"Did you ever see anything suspicious going on over there?" I feel like a third rate detective when I say this.

"No, believe it or not, I don't sit and look out the window at her place all night long. Do you think it's safe for me to stay open? I mean, if it was a burglary it could happen here next."

"Relax, Ree. Cops are all over Montrose tonight. Nothing is going to happen to another restaurant owner or to any woman in this neighborhood. Hey, you've got me and the Chief of Police in here to protect you."

She looks at me like I am her hero, and I suddenly feel better for a moment too. I feel a surge of protectiveness for her come over me. She seems so vulnerable tonight. Maybe I will spend more time with her when this is over. We did have some good times together.

When Maria moves down to the other end of the bar to greet a group of customers who are coming in, I think about what I'm doing here tonight. Suddenly I don't feel too good about being a reporter. Probing and prying and asking nosy questions are part of my life as a journalist. Now my best friend is the victim and the answers are more important than ever, but I can't get rid of a nagging voice in my head that keeps asking me if I am trying to capitalize on bad things happening to women I know.

My favorite journalism professor began every class with the same statement. The class had to repeat it like the Pledge of Allegiance. It's been twenty years but the tape still plays in my head like a Barry Manilow jingle,

"A reporter gathers information only for the benefit of readers—therefore a reporter may not make inquiries for any other purpose." Miss Saxon put special emphasis on 'any other purpose' and soon the class did too.

I've never had any problem with that premise before, but now it feels like I need to find out anything that might help to find Ginger and Darilyn. As a reporter, in theory at least, I can ask all the questions I want. The hard part is knowing what you can ask your friends.

That nagging voice in my head gets louder when I think about writing the story. I try to shut it up with logic.

"If the Times doesn't publish the story, other papers will." *It won't be my fault when people find out.*
"This is not going to stay a secret." *The public has a right to know.*
"The paper needs this story. A blockbuster story will increase our circulation." *Pete won't have to lay off any more employees.*

I take my unfinished beer and make my way back to the table when I spot our waitress delivering plates full of rollatini, shrimp scampi, and baskets of home made garlic rolls. I am just in time to overhear Frankie swearing to Nan that she has never abused Ginger and they are getting along fine. They change the subject when I sit down, and we start to talk about Darilyn.

"Carla, you were one of the last people to see Darilyn. Tell me what you can remember about last night."

Nan sounds like a police officer when she says that, and I'm wondering if she is remembering the kiss in the parking lot too. Our eyes connect for a short moment before she looks away.

"When we left, she was alone in the restaurant. Well, there were no customers but Darcy was still there. We invited Darilyn to close up early and join us at the bookstore to hear Abigail read but she said she couldn't."

I vividly recall Maria threatening Darilyn last night and wonder if I should say anything. If I don't, will Abby? I realize I have been so busy all day I have not called her. As soon as we finish eating, I excuse myself and call her before we leave the restaurant. She has checked out of the Ritz Carlton and has not left a message for me. She probably does not even know what has happened in sleepy little Montrose during her brief visit.

I have to go home to let Skip out. He has been in since I left for work early this morning. It seems like an incredibly long day to me, and I know it must to him too. I tried to coax him out from under the bed before I left for work, but he was so spooked by the thunder and lightning he wanted to stay as far away from the windows as he could get. Poor little guy, he probably thinks the booming thunder is aimed at him personally.

Nan and Frankie follow me back to my house. I have messages from my mother and Laverne. Neither sounds urgent so I will call them back tomorrow.

While Frankie makes phone calls to anyone who wasn't home during the day that she thinks may have seen Ginger, Nan and I take Skip for a walk around the block. There is a chill in the air and I don't know if I should tuck my fingers into my pocket or if I dare take Nan's hand. We are half way to the corner when I realize we are out on the streets of Montrose after dark.

"Do you have your gun? Just in case" I ask Nan.

"You've got your guard dog," she teases, but I imagine I detect a little under-tone of anxiety.

"Skip is a dog's dog but no match for a murderer or even a determined kid-napper. We are both depending on you." I reach tentatively for her hand for emphasis and hold on for warmth.

Back at my house, I bring out a cold six-pack of Heineken, and we all tiredly settle down for a talk while I light the fireplace.

"This is off the record." Nan twists open a beer and hands one to me. "Very few missing adults are the victim of any criminal activity." I'm sure her intent is to alleviate our fears. "Most missing persons show up in a few days, but if any foul play is suspected, the police investigation is escalated right away."

"But Nan, foul play should be suspected, shouldn't it? I mean, one woman murdered and two women missing at the same time…" I trail off because that is probably the reason the search for Ginger has not already officially been escalated. When the two women are single and from the same neighborhood, there is a good chance they are together.

Frankie is surprised to learn that consenting adults can be missing if they choose to. They can walk off their jobs, leave town, and disappear from their friends and family. Even if the police do locate the missing person, they won't give out any information about them unless they have permission from that person.

I know what Frankie is thinking before she says it, and so does Nan.

"So, you could know where Ginger is right now and you wouldn't tell me?"

"That's right." Nan walks over to Frankie. "If Ginger didn't give me permission to tell you where she was, I couldn't." Resting her hands lightly on Frankie's shoulders, she continues, "Not that I wouldn't want to, but the law protects her privacy."

"Okay, Nan, but what about that consenting adult part? What does that actually mean?" I ask.

"That is not so clear cut," she shrugs. "Deciding if an adult should be considered consenting sometimes is a judgment call. Generally, a missing person is considered to be consenting if he or she is eighteen."

Nan starts to pace around the room, appearing to be thinking aloud, "A few things can change that. For instance, if they have a physical or mental disability or if it can be proved they are missing involuntarily." Nan sounds as if she has made this speech numerous times to distraught husbands and wives and even parents.

They don't leave until midnight and I am exhausted, but a familiar brand of adrenaline is flowing through my veins. Nan and I are spending a lot of time together, and she seems more and more attractive to me everyday.

I know I won't be able to sleep, and if I leave now I can make it to Les Girls before last call.

The bar has a popular deejay on Friday and Saturday nights. Older women shuffling their feet and younger ones flinging their arms about share the tiny dance floor space. It takes me a few minutes to safely navigate my way to the bar. The back room has a pool table and the two big screen televisions are always turned on for the jocks that can't decide if they want to watch basketball or women's tennis.

"Mickey, my darlin'. Does your mother know you're out after dark?" The new daytime barmaid is cute, petite with spiky red hair, big green eyes, and freckles. She ended up in Detroit when she moved here from Seattle with a girlfriend who dumped her after three months. Her plans were to only work long enough to earn money to get back home to Washington, but it has been four months now and I think she may have met someone and will be staying around Motown for awhile.

We hit it off right away when Ginger introduced us. "Carla McCarthy, I'd like you to meet our new barmaid, Michelle Fitzgerald." We both started grinning that *I'm so damn happy to meet someone like me grin.* I've been promising my Mom to bring her home for a good Irish dinner. She's not my type and I'm way too old for her so there are no barriers to our being friends. Sometimes a woman is just a friend. Not an ex or a soon to be, just a friend. She is someone who makes me laugh. She noticed me sniffing her whenever we hug hello or goodbye, and she admitted she buys men's deodorant because it is cheaper. Now, she is wearing Aqua Velva after-shave in place of cologne too.

She looks at me a little quizzically. "You looking for Ginger? I've never seen you in here so late alone before."

"No, not exactly. Have you seen her?" I ask as I pull up a barstool. "She didn't show up for work at the book store last night and I just wondered if she has been sick. So many people have got the flu lately." When the words come out of my mouth, I wonder why I feel the need to lie.

"No, she wasn't here last night. The manager called me to fill in for her last night and tonight too. Gee, I hope she doesn't have the flu, or I'll probably get it too."

"If she happens to come in or calls you, give me a call, will you? It's kind of important."

Maybe I should just tell her; it's going to be all over town soon anyway. "Look Mickey, the truth is Frankie and I haven't seen or heard from Ginger. She hasn't been home and she hasn't called anyone. We are both worried about her. Ask around, will you? Just in case someone has seen her." Mickey will find out about the murder soon enough, I don't want to talk about it right now.

When I get home after two, Skip has found the doggy bag Maria sent for him, so we sit on the floor together and have a picnic with the spaghetti and meatballs. I can't keep my eyes open long enough to read even one chapter in this month's Book Club selection or any of the three days worth of the New York Times on the bedside table. I will tune in to CNN in the morning to find out what is happening in the world outside of Montrose.

I'm glad Paisley Park is already set up on the CD player next to the bed.

Ah, summer, what power you have to make us suffer and like it.

—Russell Baker (b. 1925), U.S. journalist. New York Times (27 June 1965).

Barbara Jane, RJ and Mimi Brown
Detroit
Summer 1966

One month after my little brother RJ married my best friend we took him to the airport to say good-bye. Willow Run Airport that day was full of handsome young men and weeping families. RJ was smiling like an incredibly lucky man and not one who was shipping out to Vietnam. He had two young women kissing him good-bye and promising to write everyday. His big sister, Barbara Jane Brown, tall, blond, and blue eyed, remarkably like him. The other, his dark-haired, dark-eyed, baby doll wife of four weeks, Mrs. Mimi Brown. Our entire families were there. Mom tried to smile as if she knew everything would be all right, but Mimi's mother was almost as out of control as Mimi. Dad was wearing a proud smile but he stayed close to RJ. I saw him brush shoulders with him once or twice, and I wondered if he wanted to put his arms around him. I wish he had.

The war in Vietnam was increasing in intensity, and RJ knew it was his destiny to help America win. My brother felt a special responsibility to serve his country. That is how the men in our family were. They married their high school girlfriend even if she wasn't pregnant, they drank Black Label beer, and they supported their families. It seemed there was a war for every generation. Dad served in WWII in Germany, and a few years later Uncle Mike was with the 3rd Battalion in Korea when they were ordered to Ansong. My dad came home to a hero's welcome and the GI Bill of Rights with a wife and daughter waiting. There was a framed picture of Uncle Mike in his Marine uniform on the mantel. We kept it there even at Christmas when we hung our stockings out for Santa. Mama said it was the right thing to do.

The 30 mile ride home from Willow Run airport was quiet. Mimi was making little hiccup noises and every once in a while a big noisy sniffle but she had stopped crying. Neither of us felt like talking so I turned on the radio and got

"The Ballad of the Green Berets." That made me cry too, so I turned off the radio and we drove to Mimi and RJ's house in silence.

As soon as I parked in front of their bungalow, Mimi started to cry again and moved over for a hug. I was eager to get home and be alone for awhile. "I'll see you soon, Mimi. Please don't keep crying. You'll make yourself sick."

"Please stay for dinner Barbara Jane, please, I'll cook. I can't stand to be alone right now," she pleaded. There was no sense in trying to say no to her.

Later, Mimi brought out the bottle of Blue Nun she and RJ had opened last night, and we finished it before Mimi drifted away with her head on my shoulder. The little rental house in Oak Park seemed too quiet and too empty tonight. I listened to the radio for awhile before I woke her up and went to bed.

In the next few weeks, Mimi busied herself during the day trying recipes from the red and white plaid Good Housekeeping cookbook, a wedding gift from my Aunt Martha. The older women in my family were afraid Mimi would insist on matzo ball soup, knishes, and gefilte fish for RJ. My Mother didn't say anything, but I knew she was already thinking ahead to her first grandchild. I told them they didn't need to worry. "Mimi is making stewed chicken and dumplings tonight for me, which she says 'are a lot like matzo balls anyway.'"

It was easier and easier for me to go straight to Mimi's after my nursing classes at the hospital. The table was always set with my favorite meals. Mimi teased me that she knows the way to my heart. She asks me to spend the summer with her, until she gets used to the new neighborhood.

It was sweltering hot that summer. The temperatures reached ninety degrees day after day with little relief at night. Mimi got up before I did so she could make breakfast for me. White short shorts and a polka dot halter-top were her daily uniform, and for a few brief minutes each morning, she looked cool.

Dinner preparations began as soon as I left for the hospital in the morning so the house could cool off before I come home. Nothing helped. Inside, the closed up house was like an auto factory assembly line by five o'clock when I get there. The trees and grass were scorched when the city put homeowners on a water ban for nonessential use. We were allowed two days a week to water the grass and the flowers. On those days, Mimi and I went into the backyard in our swimsuits and got wet along with the marigolds and petunias.

Mimi had made plans to start Alma's School of Cosmetology in the fall, so I was glad she had the summer to practice her home making skills. I was sure she would get tired of cooking chicken and meatloaf every night soon enough. Some nights I took her to GilliGates for fish and chips. Mimi was beginning to depend on me.

That summer seemed different without RJ. On the weekends, Mimi and I often went to the nearby Zoo and she brought a picnic basket full of southern style buttermilk fried chicken and redskin potato salad. One ninety five-degree afternoon, I played hooky and left my hospital classes two hours early, so we could drive to Belle Isle for a swim in the river before dark. We managed to find a secluded campestral spot to spread my favorite Pendleton blanket, and we both wrote letters to RJ. The car radio was tuned to WJLB and we heard "My Girl" what seemed like a dozen times that afternoon.

"I guess you'd say what can make me feel this way?
My girl, talking about my girl
I've got sunshine on a cloudy day.
When it's cold outside I've got the month of May.
I've got so much honey the bees envy me.
I've got a sweeter song than the birds in the trees.
I don't need no money, fortune, or fame.
I've got all the riches baby one man can claim.
I guess you'd say What can make me feel this way?
My girl (my girl, my girl) Talkin' 'bout my girl (my girl).

Mimi insisted the Baby Doll pajamas she bought for her honeymoon were the only things cool enough for her to wear to bed. I just kept wearing the Tigers tee shirt I have been wearing since junior high.

There was only one double bed. Before Mimi's marriage in June, we were both used to sleeping alone. It was so hot and humid that summer I offered to sleep on the couch every night, but Mimi inexplicably insisted we sleep together. During the heat wave, I learned a trick from one of the nurses at the hospital, and I couldn't wait to try it out. Mimi and I sat on the porch after dinner for awhile looking at the stars and listening to the Tigers play the White Sox at Wrigley Field. Al Kaline looked a lot like RJ so we always rooted for him. Mimi told me with my short summer haircut and my favorite red baseball cap I looked like Al Kaline too. We drank a couple of cold Miller Lights before were tired enough to go into the steamy aluminum frame house.

After the lights were off and the noisy window fan was lazily blowing thick warm air on us; I told Mimi I had a surprise for her. "Take your nightshirt off for a minute while I go in the kitchen and get it for you. It's dark, no one will see you." I made her cover her eyes when I came back in the room. I hoped I wouldn't trip over someone's shoes and spoil the surprise. "OK, move your arms and legs like you are making a snow angel and imagine how cold the snow is," I told her feeling only a little foolish. When I put the first cold plastic bottle under her right arm, she gasped and her eyes flew open. When I put the second pop bottle under her left arm, she giggled and tucked it close to her side. The next two bottles were directed under her knees. We laughed when I accidentally touched her and made silly jokes to cover up our nervousness.

"I always heard you were frigid"
"What a friend—did you have to get red pop?"
"Oh, I forgot you like Fresca."
"I'm not drinking this stuff tomorrow"
"Oh, yeah…you'll get so hot; you'll be begging me for a drink."
'Well, if it gets any hotter, I may not want to share.'

For awhile that night, we were kids again. By morning, childhood was over.

That was the beginning of a new phase of our relationship.

For three weeks, my wishes came wildly, exuberantly true. We spent every moment together, watching television, holding hands, shyly kissing good morning. We told ourselves we were saving water by showering together. We slept naked and slept deeply. The genie had escaped from the jar and we couldn't put her back again.

The heat broke when it rained for three days and nights. The first night she taught me mahjong. We went to bed early and the susurrant drumming of the rain brought vividly sensual dreams. I taught her poker the next while the rain threatened to wash away her fledgling tomato and cucumber garden. The third night we brought out the old Monopoly game RJ and Mama had played while my father and I watched the Friday night fights. It brought back so many memories of RJ. The realization hit me that he had gone to war and might not be coming back.

I felt so alone that night. I had never been a sister without a brother nearby before. There was an emptiness that was bigger than I could have imagined. I couldn't pretend that RJ needed me to take care of him any more. When we got in bed, Mimi hugged me for a long time before we said good night. A cool night breeze created a chill in the room, and we had to look for the sheet to cover us. Some time after midnight, the chill reached under the thin cotton sheet and moved us instinctively closer. When her breasts touched my back and her arm imprisoned me, I awoke for a moment.

That night I dreamed RJ and I were kids again shooting hoops with my Dad when suddenly RJ was dressed in camouflage fatigues and was shooting a rifle at me and Dad. I screamed when I realized the basketball rebounding towards him was on fire.

I hated the war, I even hated the president, and I wished everything could be like it was before. I was so confused; it felt as if I were RJ living here with his wife. She treated me like RJ. Maybe we were both pretending so we didn't have to face the truth that he was in Vietnam and the pictures on the nightly news were real.

Did I love Mimi? Yes, of course. How would it have ended if the phone hadn't rung at six o'clock on the morning of August 1st? I don't know. I'll never know because the phone did ring and RJ had been killed in action.

"Star Bright, Star Light, First Star I see tonight, wish I may, wish I might have the wish I wish…"

Carla McCarthy
Montrose
Saturday Morning, Sept. 9, 2000

I call a couple of Ginger's exes, that Frankie doesn't need to know about, in case she is with one of them. She isn't, but they are both concerned and promise to call me if they hear from her.

Before I can set the phone down, it rings and I see from the caller ID it is Maria.

"Hi, gorgeous. That rollatini was awesome last night. Is everything okay?"

"Hi, Babe. Yes, everything is okay, I guess. I was glad to see you last night but what I'd really like to know is why you and Frankie Q. were having dinner with Nan Lawson. You never did explain. I know it wasn't just for the rollatini. Were you checking up on me?"

"Come on, Ree. You can figure it out. We were talking about the murder and Darilyn." I know it will be impossible to divert her from this conversation, so I might as well dive right in.

"Do the police think it was a robbery attempt? Do they have any suspects yet?"

"I don't know, Maria. I may as well tell you, Ginger is missing too, and that was my main concern when I was talking to Nan."

"Ginger is missing too?" Maria repeats incredulously. "Oh, no. I can't believe it. Was she involved with Darilyn?"

"Why would you even ask me that? Look, I can't talk any more right now. I've got some things to do. Skip says thanks for the doggy bag."

I promise to keep in touch, even though we usually see each other only when I go to the restaurant or when she phones me desperate for a fourth for poker. Lately, I haven't been able to afford either the meals at the Italian Café or the high stake poker games her friends prefer. She must be shook up to be calling me first thing on a Saturday morning. The Maria I remember never got out of bed before noon.

As soon as I feed Skip and the cats, I get out the mink oil to condition my new leather boots. When I start a load of laundry, I realize I am procrastinating. I have to get out of the house and look for Ginger. She is not going to show up on my doorstep, and even if she does, she has a key to get in.

Before I go, I want to see what the suburban section of the Detroit Free Press has to say about Montrose. I'll be surprised if there is even one paragraph on the murdered woman. It is the weekend and in all likelihood, there have been several homicides in Detroit. One more in Montrose probably won't even make the paper. There might be something on Darilyn D'Angelo but I doubt if they have anything about Ginger yet. A missing barmaid is not news in Detroit. The owner of a restaurant might be.

I pour one last cup of coffee and take a cinnamon roll out of the breadbox to help me focus before I check the headlines. First page, second section! Holy shit! I can't believe my eyes! It's the slick chick in the brown silk from Laverne's last week. The article identifies her as thirty-year-old Belinda Norton, wife of wealthy businessman Jeremy Norton. This picture was taken a few years ago, but I am sure it is her. Of course! She matches the description Marge gave me yesterday! She was being politically correct by not mentioning the victim was black. The property loss of a wealthy man will make news when the disappearance of single women will not.

I don't know if I should call Nan or Pete first. Habit wins out and when I get Pete on the phone, all I can say is "Where the hell are the pictures from the book store? She's in them."

Pete calms me down a little until I am coherent enough to tell him the woman who was murdered was at the First Thursday event. As he is yelling around his office for someone to get him a Free Press, I'm surprised by how flustered he sounds. After I reassure Pete that I am absolutely, positively certain it is the same woman, he sounds uneasy because he can't remember what he did with my roll of film. The murder in Montrose has eclipsed his interest in the Mayor's race. He promises to find the film, and I hurriedly hang up and then call Chief Lawson. I am disciplining myself to think of her as Chief Lawson when I talk to her about the criminal investigation and think of her as Nan only when she is out of uniform.

I am hoping Nan will be in the office and she is. While I had been lying in bed thinking, Nan has been in the office working since seven. The Chief uncharacteristically listens to my story without any interruptions. When I pause for air, she wants to know where the roll of film is now. I hear her sigh of frustration when I tell her I left it at the Times with Pete Brown and he is currently having the lab there develop it. If there are any good photographs, I know Pete will want to run them.

Before I can leave the house, the doorbell rings. My first instinct is to hide. The only people it can be on Saturday are those husband and wife teams who go door to door in order to save your immortal soul. I made the mistake of letting them in one summer years ago and it took me till Thanksgiving to get them out. There should be a law against them. All over America, people have to hide in their own homes. I wish I had the gumption to just go to the door and say no thank you to whatever they want to give me.

"Carla, I know you are in there. Let me in, it's Laverne." Skip is dancing with anticipation and he can't hold in a few welcoming yips and arfs. Somehow, he knows who it is. I wish he had told me it was a friend.

"You didn't return my call last night, so I thought I might as well come over here. Today is Shirley's morning to work at the store." Laverne pours herself a cup of coffee but remains standing in the kitchen. "I promise not to stay long, but I would like to talk to you about Darilyn and Ginger."

I glance at my watch and nod. "Take as long as you want. I'm on my way in to see Nan. I could have met you at the bookstore and saved you a drive over here."

"I needed this to be private. At least for right now. Shirley doesn't know about this and I'm hoping she won't have to."

"Okay, you've got me curious now. Start talking."

"Before Darilyn opened the restaurant, she stopped into the bookstore and introduced herself to me. Shirley was out with her knee surgery so I was alone in the store a lot during that time. There was a lot of snow and icy rain at that time and some days there wasn't a customer all afternoon. Darilyn would come in with a bottle of her homemade wine and we would sip and chat or I would make tea for us in the microwave. She's a wonderful listener and I probably talked too much. Sometimes Jane would drop in with egg rolls or mooncakes, and we would have a little picnic right in the middle of the bookstore."

"So what does Ginger have to do with this?"

"Well, nothing, really, except…one evening after I closed up, the three of us were joking about going to get a room. One thing led to another. Nothing that has anything to do with Ginger."

This was a twist I never expected. Laverne wouldn't meet my eyes, but she kept talking.

"Our friendship, if you could call it that, blossomed during the summer. We got together occasionally when all of us happened to be free on the same night."

"Recently Jane asked me to call Ginger to join us. I think Darilyn said something about threesomes being fun but four was fairer. I'd had a couple of glasses of wine and I can't be sure whose idea it was to call her. Jane clearly has a crush on her, but Darilyn seemed anxious to meet her too for her own reasons."

"Look, I know China Jane pretty well; we used to play softball together. She knows Ginger is my best friend. She never mentioned having a crush on her to me. When was all of this?"

"It was two weeks ago. Shirley and I have been having some problems, and I needed to get away and relieve the stress, so I made plans to spend the evening with some female friends. Darilyn and Jane were there."

I have to sit down. My head is swimming with pictures that I never imagined before. Laverne is so much the stereotypical old maid English teacher. I think I must have misunderstood the implications. A threesome? With Jane and Darilyn? No wonder she doesn't want Shirley to know.

"Look, Carla. Please try to understand. It was just a summer fling. I was going to call it off and try to work things out with Shirley. I knew it couldn't last. I love Shirley and would never want to hurt her. You can tell Nan if you have to, but no one else, please. Shirley has a jealous streak and if she knew about Darilyn, she might say things she doesn't mean."

"Why are you telling me this now? I still don't see what it has to do with Ginger or even Darilyn's disappearance. I admit, it's interesting gossip but nothing I think Nan needs to know."

"Something strange happened that night. We were in Darilyn's private office at the restaurant after she closed and we all heard an unusual noise. It sounded like someone was at the back door."

"How frightening. Was there actually someone there?"

"Darilyn got up to turn on the lights but by the time she did the sound had stopped. It seemed to come from the wall connecting Vegelina's to the store owned by the gay guys next door."

"What did you do?"

"We just made a joke of it but the mood was ruined and Jane and I left shortly after. I never called Ginger."

"Did you ever find out who or what it was?"

"There was a man in the parking lot but he moved away too quickly when we came out to get a good look at him. Now I wonder if it was someone who was setting up a robbery and Belinda got caught at the wrong place, at the wrong time."

"Laverne, you are blowing my mind. Did you warn Darilyn? Can you describe the man at all?"

"I told Darilyn about it the next day but none of us took it seriously. We even laughed that it was probably a pervert who had seen the three of us together and was hoping for an invitation to join us."

When Laverne leaves, I try to make sense of it. I know she has been under a lot of stress and Shirley's health problems have been difficult for both of them to deal with. I'm sure she felt she could confide in me because she knows I won't make any moral judgments.

I wonder if Laverne's secret is still a secret, or if she was playing too close to home.

By the time I get to Montrose, it is already one o'clock. My first stop is at the police station to see Nan. When I walk into Headquarters, the Chief's door is closed, and Mike shakes his head when I gesture that I want to go in. "Conference call with the Chiefs," he confides. Detroit, Southfield, and Montrose Police Chiefs are pooling information and coordinating resources. The victim lived in Rosedale Park, an upscale community in Detroit just 15 miles west of Montrose, and Southfield borders Montrose on the east. Southfield is an ethnically diverse community whose claim to fame is that it is home to the first urban mall in America. Felons from other communities often flee to the anonymity of Southfield thinking everyone looks alike in a mall if it is big enough.

When I eventually get in to see the Chief, we talk for a long time about the event at the Book Store. "Carla, tell me everything you remember about Belinda Norton and who she was talking to," Nan asks as she takes out a pen and paper from her top drawer.

"You must have seen Belinda yourself. Maybe you just didn't notice her. She was the woman who was talking to Abby for quite a while after the reading, and that is the reason I have her photo." Nan is nodding as if she remembers, so I continue. "I noticed she was very pretty and had a lot of gold jewelry on. I was trying to get some good candids of Ms Carr alone but she and Belinda were having a long conversation until Belinda noticed me taking photographs and moved away."

Nan calls Abby's service and tells them it is an urgent police matter. They promise to page her while Nan holds. When Abigail picks up, Nan identifies herself and asks if it is all right if she puts her on speaker and she records the call. Abby's first response is, "Do I need a lawyer?" which I think is strange, but the Chief is probably used to people saying things like that to her.

Abigail doesn't sound relieved to know that I am in the room. When Nan asks her, about who she may have met or talked to at Laverne and Shirley's on September 7, Abigail says she rarely remembers people from book signings. She remembers Laverne and Shirley, she remembers me, of course, and she remembers the phone ringing incessantly. She remembers the Mayor was there but that is about it.

"Ms Carr, the evening in question was less than 48 hours ago. I am conducting a police investigation here. Please tell me what you remember."

"There were a lot of people there, no one particular person stands out. I'm sorry; I would like to help you if I could. What happened, if I may ask?"

With a permissive nod from the Chief, I ask her, "Abigail, you must remember talking to a pretty woman dressed in a gorgeous, dark brown silk pants suit wearing a lot of gold jewelry?"

After a slight pause, she admits that Bebe drove her back to her hotel suite in Dearborn that night. So, that is what her other plans were! Bebe! Isn't that too too sweet! I can't believe it; I thought she and I had something going on. So that is why she didn't call me…A million thoughts are running through my head. The ones that aren't angry are hurt. But almost all are angry.

"We have reason to believe the woman you were talking to was Belinda Norton who was murdered between midnight Thursday and 4:00 Friday morning. You are one of the last people to have seen her alive."

At this point, the Chief takes the phone off speaker and asks me to leave the room for a few minutes. I wander around the waiting room looking at the FBI's Ten Most Wanted posters for awhile, make a quick round trip to the ladies' room, and she is still on the phone. After what seems like hours, Nan opens her office door and beckons me back in.

"Sorry, Carla. I needed to speak to her confidentially."

"Did you find anything out? What's going on with them? You don't think Abigail did it, do you?"

"Carla, you need to slow down. Obviously, nothing is going on with them. Mrs. Norton is dead and Abigail will call me if she remembers anything else about that evening. We have several leads we are working on even as we speak. I assure you we are investigating everyone who saw Mrs. Norton that evening."

Nan opens a desk drawer and takes out a thick folder as she points a chewed up wooden pencil at me. "That includes you, my hot-tempered Irish friend. Where were you when you left the bookstore?"

"Do you honestly want me to answer that?"

She surprises me with an unprecedented mischievous wink. "Get out of here before you perjure yourself. I wouldn't want to have to lock you up."

The Chief is clearly finished with me for the moment. I leave after we agree to meet for a sandwich at the Coney about six. It's easier to leave my car in the lot at the police station and walk the few blocks downtown. My new Sketchers have not had a good workout yet, plus I could use the exercise. No sense in competing with the weekend shoppers for a parking space. Dinah often draws a crowd, and I don't want to have grimy kid handprints on her. She will be happier waiting for me at the police station.

In the meantime, I am determined to redeem myself with Nan. The first thing I can do is to start making the rounds of potential witnesses up and down 9 Mile Rd. The police have already canvassed both sides of the street. Montrose has more than its share of restaurants for a small town, and it is building a reputation for funky clothing stores as well as music and bookstores too.

Vegelina's is on the northeast corner; next to it is Clark's Closet, a vintage clothing store. I became friendly with Randy and Ray when we worked on an Aids HIV fundraiser two years ago. They donated a 1920 Gatsby era pastel suit as well as some less pricey items, and I poured $10 glasses of Merlot and auto-graphed customized Horoscopes. The guys were my best customers, and together our two booths raised $900. Their store closes at seven on Thursday nights, and they didn't recall seeing or hearing anything out of the ordinary that night. Of course, they are all atwitter contemplating a stalker in the neighborhood and are sure they will be next. They change the erasable sign on the door and declare they will close at six every night until spring when day light savings returns and it will stay light later.

The next three stops are even less fruitful. The Magic Store is owned by a nice, roly-poly little man with a big droopy mustache and dark curling hair on the backs of his stubby hands all the way to his knuckles. I had written an article about Mr. Hawkins and his magical store last year for the Times, and he swears he has me to thank for an upsurge in his usually slow summer business. He insists on showing me a new card trick called The Disappearing Lady. He turns four Queens into three Queens and one Jack, but he regretfully doesn't know anything about Darilyn or Ginger's disappearance. "Don't worry about me. Not all of the guns in here shoot blanks," Hawk offers with a grim smile as I leave.

Mr. and Mrs. Goodnights is owned by a lesbian friend. We wrote a series of articles together about the Telecom industry for Newsweek when she worked at MCI in the '80's. When she got the boot on Black Thursday in 1985 along with 4,000 others, she took her savings and her generous severance package and opened this store. While she is busy helping a customer select scented candles for the perfect bedtime ambiance, I look around at the cute but pricey pure cotton pajamas and nightshirts. When Leslie has time to talk to me, it is more gossip than any real information. She says that Darilyn stopped in a few times and made big purchases: New Age music CDs, aromatherapy lotions and oils, and a set of silk sheets. Leslie has been single for a long time, and I think she was hoping a romance might have been brewing with the attractive and apparently available Darilyn. She asks me to promise to call her if I find out anything. I agree to call her for dinner soon and keep going.

The third storefront is used for seasonal rentals. From November to the end of the year, a Christmas home décor and collectibles store sets up shop. Income Tax preparers move in starting in January and the LGBT crowd takes over for Pride fund raising activities in June. Right now, in September, it appears empty although I check the door just in case someone is inside remodeling for the next tenants. Witches, ghosts, George Bush, Hilary Clinton, and a few movie stars will be moving in by the first of October along with various axe murderers, black cats, and goblins. No luck so I move along.

The Tool Shed and Ted's Barber Shop are so testosterone loaded I don't bother to go in. I'll leave that to Montrose's finest. The Broadway is on the corner so I take a break and stop in. The waitress seems surprised when I just want coffee. I tell her I have to save my appetite so I can eat with Nan at six.

The Saturday afternoon shopping and lunch crowds are still in town. It's mostly young families getting haircuts for the kids or Dad looking for tools while Mom gets a manicure or shops at the Drug Mart. They will either have lunch at the Broadway Deli or take out some egg rolls and fried rice from China Jane's and be on their way home before dark. A few senior citizens have walked over from Evergreen Towers to enjoy the late summer sunshine and find a convenient bench to sit on and watch the shoppers go by. In a few hours, a whole new crowd will arrive when the Saturday night dinner date couples descend looking for parking spaces.

My next stop is the bookstore. I hope that Laverne is not there yet. I am curious about what Shirley will say. She is with a customer when I arrive and gives me a sign to wait and not leave.

"The police were here yesterday asking about the murdered woman and Darilyn," Shirley tells me as soon as the customer leaves.

"Frankie and I still have not heard from Ginger."

Shirley doesn't look surprised at that. I wonder if she knows something she is not telling me.

"I guess the police will be back asking questions about her, too. Carla, if people are afraid to come here this could ruin our business." Shirley is rubbing her temples as if she can rub away what is happening. "I didn't want to say anything about the police being here in front of that customer."

Shirley's pale blue eyes are weepy looking and I am afraid she is ready to cry. I wonder how much she knows about Laverne's summer madness. I don't know how to console her because I know her fear is real, not only for the missing women, but for her business and marriage too. I've seen what crime and the fear of crime has done in areas of Detroit that were once vibrant shopping areas just a few miles from Montrose.

Laverne and Shirley have sunk their retirement savings into this place. Shirley confided in me one night after a couple of drinks that the stock market slide had jeopardized their plans for a Florida condominium and the easy beach life they wanted. She usually wasn't the kind to complain, so I knew things must be tight. The pain of her two knee surgeries and the long recovery time added to their problems.

I give her what I hope is a reassuring hug. "Don't worry, we'll find both of them. You know they might be together and just forgot to call. This whole thing will probably blow over in a couple of days."

Shirley throws her arms in the air with frustration. "Carla, get a grip, stop living in denial. A woman is dead. She was here at 10 o'clock at night and before the next morning, she was dead! This is not going to blow over. Ginger is in danger. So are we!"

There are dark circles under Shirley's eyes and the frown lines seem deeper around her mouth. This situation is aging all of my friends very fast. I didn't even look in the mirror this morning; it is probably aging me too.

Before I leave, I buy a new Melissa Etheridge CD and a couple of chocolate truffles they keep by the cash register for impulse buyers like me. As I make my way across the street, I dodge a SUV full of eight-year old cub scouts popping their heads out of the windows. The driver is attempting to talk on the phone and make an illegal U-turn at the same time.

On the corner is a Drug Mart, which is as large and impersonal as any national chain store. I go in, look around in a desultory fashion, and when I pick up a USA Today, I notice there are not any Candid Times in the rack. As I pay the cashier, I ask her if they have sold out of the Times because of the front-page articles on the missing women. If the pink streaks in her blond hair are meant to indicate she is the type of girl who likes to have fun, she has for-gotten they are there. "I'm not sure why we ran out so soon," she replies grudg-ingly "but we do usually have some Candid Times left over. I've got a copy behind the counter if you want to look at it." As I shake my head no thanks and start to leave, she adds, "My boyfriend is going to be picking me up after work from now on. I never thought there would be a killer in Montrose."

"Have you seen this woman?" I show her a picture of Ginger crossing the finish line at a MACS 5K run.

"She's not the dead woman. Is she a suspect? Why are you looking for her?"

All of a sudden, this young girl has me explaining myself. I always feel guilty about something. I must still be paying off a karmic debt for something I did in another lifetime.

"No, she is not a suspect. She is a friend of mine and I haven't seen her for a couple of days. With everything that is going on in Montrose, I'm just worried about her. I thought she might have stopped in here."

"Are you with the cops?"

"No, Ginger is a friend of mine. My best friend actually. I'm not with the police but I do work for the Candid Times. My name is Carla McCarthy. Here is my card. Please call me if you hear or see anything."

"Okay, I'll help you out if I can. A lot of weirdos come in here, especially at night, if you know what I mean. My name is Asia. You know, like the country."

"Nice to meet you Asia. If you can't get me, just leave a message and I'll get back to you as soon as I can."

When I come out with my newspaper under my arm and a Reese's Peanut Butter Cup in my pocket, the aroma of shrimp fried rice and spring rolls is wafting out from China Jane's. I wish I had asked Nan to meet me there for dinner. There is something about the smell of Chinese food that makes me hungry any time of the day.

I can see the McGuire twins waving at me through the windows at Tootsie's. Today must be perm day; they both have little pink rods in their bleached blond hair. One of these days, their hair is going to fall out. I wave back before I realize they are trying to wave me over.

"Good afternoon, ladies," usually works well with them. They know most people can't tell them apart. It would help if one of them would lose weight.

"If you see Tootsie, please tell her to come back here and check on us," wails Penny from behind a Glamour magazine. "She said she would be right back and it has been almost an hour," comes from Patty. I'm relieved to see they have their names embroidered on their matching cardigans.

"Sure, I'll keep an eye open for her," I promise, hoping Tootsie isn't going to be the next woman missing.

There is no time for me to start worrying about her whereabouts. Tootsie is right next door at China Jane's waiting for a take out. "Excuse me, Tootsie?" She was so intent on reading the headline story in the Times; she didn't notice me at first. "The McGuire sisters are looking for you, something about their hair?"

Tootsie straightens the blond wig she is wearing today, and furtively says something to Jane, and leaves abruptly without speaking to me.

"Carla, the police just left here asking me about a murder at Vegelina's Thursday night." Jane pushes her glasses to the top of her head as she stands up and walks towards me. "They said they are looking for Darilyn and Ginger Harris too."

"Yes, I know," I admit. "Didn't you know about it?"

"The woman who was murdered? No, I didn't come to work yesterday. I had an appointment downtown at the VA so I took the day off. Went home and went to bed early, I just needed to catch up on my sleep I guess."

"Are you and Tootsie worried?"

"Worried about what? We didn't have anything to do with the murder. It was probably her husband or boyfriend who killed her." Jane leans on the counter, "Fortunately, I don't have any of those kinds of problems," she said with shrug, "and neither does Tootsie."

"Can I get a pot of tea, Jane, and a couple of moon cakes?" I promise myself that I'll have a small dinner tonight to make up for the truffles and cakes.

"Are you here to eat McCarthy, or ask questions for the paper?" Jane asks as she wipes her hands on a soy sauce stained towel by the sink.

"I was in town and just thought you might have time to talk for a few minutes," I answer when she delivers my pot of tea. "You know Ginger and I are best friends and I'm worried sick about her," I said as I open a Sweet and Low to put in my tea. "Apparently she was on her way to the bookstore Thursday night but never made it," I continue. "Since I found out a woman was murdered the same night I'm frantic. I just thought maybe you had seen her."

"Ginger may have had a date that night that lasted longer than she expected. Of course, I'm concerned about her, but I don't know Darilyn very well. How do we know she didn't do it? I mean, the murder happened in her restaurant. I'm glad it didn't happen here. Like I said before, the woman who was murdered was probably killed by her husband."

"I would believe that if Ginger and Darilyn weren't both missing too" I replied, nodding at least partial agreement. "Even if he killed her in a state of jealous rage, I'm pretty sure she wasn't dating both Darilyn and Ginger! And why would he take them someplace? There weren't any signs of other bodies in the restaurant, as far as I know."

Jane gets up abruptly. "I say everybody should just mind their own business. It's no one's business who is dating who, who is drinking too much, and who is jealous of who. I'm going to stay out of it and I'm sure Laverne is doing the same thing."

Her lies are making me feel uncomfortable. Why won't she admit she knows Darilyn very well? Or is Laverne lying to cover up something?

Jane looks agitated and I think I better leave. As I walk out, I remember that Jane has a softball game tomorrow at Clark Park. I feel sad remembering there was a time not long ago we would have been going there together.

There is a CLOSED sign on the front door at Vegelina's. I take the time to talk to some of the employees in nearby shops.

"How's business?" "*A robbery, that's terrible.*"
"How come Vegelina's is closed on a Saturday night?" "*A murder? Really?*"
"Who was the victim?" "*Naked?*"
"Do you know what happened to the woman who runs Vegelina's?" "*The FBI is investigating?*" "*She has been kidnapped!*" "*Held for ransom?*"

The only thing that surprises me is how many people know and apparently like Darilyn.

When I meet Nan at the Coney Island, she is still in uniform, which means she was going back to work. As soon as we find an empty booth and sit down, she starts talking about the case. "I told the duty sergeant to assign extra cars to patrol the parking lots on both sides of the street tonight. We'll have a couple of officers on mountain bikes in the downtown business district also." I give up on any personal conversation when she continues, "We will keep extra cars circulating in the surrounding neighborhoods tonight too."

After the waitress takes our Coney orders, "extra onions, chili and mustard and large root beers please," I tell Nan what I've heard on the street today. "Rumors are circulating that Darilyn shot an intruder and panicked and she is hiding out. The other popular theory is there was a robbery attempt and the robber's accomplices took her hostage."

We are both glad when our food comes, and we can stop talking about this for at least a few minutes.

When we're finished with the Detroit style dogs, I hesitantly try to be nurturing. "Nan you must be exhausted. Why don't you go home and get some rest? You have a great team. I know they are doing everything possible."

Before I can even get all of the words out, she gives me that gorgonizing look she is infamous for.

"There is one woman dead and two women missing from the same area on the same night. In my town! I was a block away from where it happened, Carla, and so were you. Do you honestly think I can rest? That I should rest? I don't need to tell you that every minute counts in a case like this. Ginger is your best friend. I would think you would want me spending every minute looking for her."

"You're right as usual. That's why you're the police chief and I'm just the reporter."

I have to try to appease her. "You know I want a story, but of course I want Ginger back even more. Is there something, anything I can do to help? You are working so hard."

Nan dials down the scorching gorgon look to warm. "Thanks, Carla. Some people may talk to you who won't talk to the police. Just keep doing what you have been doing. Talk to anybody and everybody who might know something. Just don't forget to let me know if you turn up anything. You can call me day or night on my private line."

She is half way out the door when I catch up with her to get a ride back to the station for my car. When she pulls up next to my car in the nearly empty lot, her sense of humor has returned. Instead of the curt goodbye that I expected, she says, "Carla, it's important to me to work hard. It's better than being afraid."

"You never seem to be afraid of anything."

"Have you forgotten what John Lennon said? 'Work is life, you know, and without it, there's nothing but fear.'"

I think we are forming a real bond during this crisis. I love her professionalism and her easy confidence. She is layered like a tasty Greek baklava. The crusty top layer may be police officer but the sweet, honey layer underneath is a poet. We've been together three nights in a row since Thursday night. I can't help but wonder if there is a future for us when this is over.

By early evening, word has gotten around to the waitresses, cooks and bar staff in Montrose that Ginger Harris, the popular blonde bartender at Les Girls, is missing too. Employees who have to work until closing time Saturday night form little support groups to walk to their cars together. People have not panicked yet but they are definitely apprehensive. I know when the public finds out there are now three women dead or missing there is going to be a panic. One woman missing is one thing, but I think a lot of people are trying to rationalize that as long as it was a robbery, they are safe. So many people don't even read newspapers but only catch the morning or evening local television news. They may not even be aware that the other women have not been found yet.

Before I go to bed, I check for any new email messages and then log onto the web to see what I can find out about Darilyn D'Angelo and Belinda Norton. I figure I may as well Google the restaurants Darilyn worked at in London and Vancouver while I am on line.

I found a connection to Darilyn in Vancouver. An old college chum lives there and actually knew Darilyn. Leesa is another ex who thinks I should never be interested in anyone but her, no matter how long it has been. She was willing to admit she knew Darilyn when she found out I was not interested in her for personal reasons, but she isn't willing to tell me very much about her on the phone.

"Leesa, the police are looking for Darilyn. She has been missing since Thursday night. A young woman was found murdered in her restaurant early Friday morning."

"Oh my God, do they think she did it?" is her first response, which surprises me.

"I don't think so," I hedge a bit. "I think the police are afraid she and Ginger are victims too."

After that bombshell, she barrages me with non-stop questions that I try to answer succinctly so she will realize how serious the situation is. She promises to call me back in an hour after checking flights from Vancouver to Detroit.

In twenty minutes, she has cleared a couple of days off from the chiropractic clinic with her partner and secured a cat sitter for Oliver. When she calls me back, she is packing and says she will be here as soon as possible. I have no choice but to give her my cell phone number. I can always get it changed if things don't work out.

I lie in bed thinking about life for awhile before I fall asleep. While I was waiting for Leesa to call me back, out of my wretched curiosity I look up Abigail Carr and that high-toned boarding school she went to. I find out more than I want to.

As I fall asleep, I listen to my new Melissa CD, and think about love lost and love found.

"War Song"

—*Neil Young Lyrics*

In the morning when you wake up
You've got planes flying in the sky
Flying bombs made to break up
All the lies in your eyes

BJ Brown
Fort Sam Houston
September 1966

Even today, I can't recall the actual details of my life in the weeks after my brother was killed. All I can recall are the feelings. I needed to be alone; I couldn't face my Mother and Father's grief with my guilt. I didn't know what Mimi expected of me. The sympathy her widowhood clothed her in erased her from me. Our families and friends surrounded her. Her Mother insisted she come home and stay with them. She was the widow, I was just the sister. There was no place for me in her life now. There wasn't any place for me anymore.

After RJ's funereal, I didn't want anyone ever to call me Barbara Jane again. When I walked into the recruitment office, I requested and got an official name change on my military records. Maybe they saw my family records; maybe they just saw the look in my eyes. Maybe they would say or do anything to get trained nurses to Vietnam. By my first week in Basic Training at Fort Sam Houston, I was BJ Brown. Boot Camp did not reward women for anything soft or feminine.

Basic Training was a blur. I resented the days off, the women who wanted to be my friends, the invitations to share a beer at the end of a long day. If there were any feelings of fear or loneliness, I piled hours of study and hard physical exercise on top of them like coats on a bed to make them disappear. Work was my valued companion, the only friend I needed now.

During those weeks, I was consumed with an urgent need to get to Vietnam. I wanted to breathe the air Bobby breathed, I wanted to see the train tracks where the ambush took place, I wanted to lie on the ground where he bled to death. He was no longer RJ to me. He was the little brother Bobby who lived with me in those halcyon years in Missouri when it was just the two of us, and we had never moved to Michigan or heard of anyone like Mimi.

My sleep during those weeks was dreamless. My soul seemed to be in between realities, and I kept my brain too tired to remember the past or imagine the future.

At the end of six weeks I had marched hundreds of miles, I could competently read a compass and a map, and I was on my way to becoming an officer in the US Army. I was determined to forget I was a sister with no brother, but I would always remember I was a woman who would not ask for nor deserve forgiveness.

Lt. BJ Brown couldn't marry her high school sweetheart, no family depended on her for support, but she could be the first woman in her family to serve in the military. I could defend my country.

I don't know if Mom and Dad ever knew I finished at the top of my class. I didn't tell them.

Carla McCarthy
Detroit
Sunday Sept 10, 2000

I can think just as well while I am cleaning litter pans. On Sundays, the MACS animal shelter is open from ten until three. Instead of going to church, I put on some old jeans and a sweat-shirt, and head over to Mac Dougall Avenue. I don't expect to see Ginger there but maybe she has called.

"Carla, it's good to see you here this morning." George offers his hand for a firm handshake or as a prelude to a hug, whichever you're in the mood for. Today I need a hug. "Where is your buddy Ginger?"

"I don't know where she is, George." I shrug uneasily. "I thought she might be here this morning. She hasn't been at work for a couple of nights."

Everyone here this Sunday morning is a volunteer. I'm glad to see 'Big George' Anderson here organizing the newer volunteers who show up but don't have a clue what needs to be done. During the week, he is the maintenance man at Northern High School. At six foot three and the combined weight of George Foreman and two or three George Juniors, he looks like a person to be taken seriously. He does a good job of getting the volunteers to do what needs to be done but his real skill is in calming frightened animals. Sometimes a rescue crew will call him at home to see if he is available during the week to ride along with them to pick up an injured dog. Some of the big dogs don't come willingly. Even if they are too sick or weak to struggle, they are often too heavy for one person to pick up. George just looks at them and starts talking to them in his deep, dark, rich voice and they calm right down. When he touches a hurt animal, his hands are so gentle; you can see the animal relaxing as he checks them over for injuries.

Ginger spends several days a month volunteering here. Days when I am feeling upbeat and emotionally strong, I will spend a few hours with her at the shelter. I know she would like me to go with her more often, but I just cannot right now. I have had three wonderful companions that all came from the shelter. I would like to take every one of the homeless animals home with me. I have tried to explain to her how hard it is for me. She says she would like to feel sorry for me, but she doesn't have any sympathy left when she leaves here. I think she donates more money to the Shelter than she makes in tips at the bar. Animals have always seemed more important to her than money. She still resents her family for not allowing her to have a pet when she was growing up.

My three hour shift flies by, but it is hard to resist taking home two adorable calico kittens. I remember to put my name on the Volunteer time sheet so if Ginger comes in she will see that I have been here.

When I'm back in the car, I remember I haven't eaten yet today and dinner won't be until five o'clock. I call Ginger's house to see if Frankie wants to meet me for lunch but she doesn't want to leave the house. She is sure Ginger will come home any minute. There is a fast food drive-through close to her, so I offer to pick up some burgers and fries and go over there. I need to talk to someone and Frankie sounds like she does, too. I get two of everything on the dollar menu for me and Frankie, and I order two plain burgers to share with Buster and Scotty. They deserve some comfort food.

The possibility that the two women are together on some extended fool-hardy lesbian honeymoon is still high on my wish list of possibilities, but I don't want to say that to Frankie. She and I try to remember if we have ever seen Ginger talking to Darilyn before.

Buster has planted himself as close as he can get to me on the couch, and Scotty is on my lap trying his best to kiss me. I try to convince them one French fry at a time their Mother is coming back, and they never have to worry about going back to the shelter.

"As far as I know, Ginger has never shown any interest in vegetarian cuisine of any kind. She doesn't even give these guys veggies." I give Scotty a pickle to prove a point, and he spits it out. "Skip loves tomatoes and carrot sticks, not as much as French fries and a burger, but he likes them. I wonder how he would like tofu from Vegelina's."

Frankie nodded her head. "I can hardly get her to eat a salad. Ginger would rather have a chili dog and onion rings from the Coney Island or even calamari from Maria's place."

"I actually like the vegetables and tofu at Vegelina's, but I wouldn't try to get Ginger to go there," I add remembering my recent dinner at Vegelina's with Abigail feeling more melancholy than I am comfortable with.

When a couple of hours of fruitless speculation pass and still no phone call from Ginger, I have to leave. My mother is expecting me for dinner at five and I don't want to disappoint her. Today is Irish stew day, one dish that all of the kids and grandkids like.

Clark Park is on the way to my mother's if I go the long way past old Tiger Stadium. A play-off game is scheduled today for the women's league Jane plays fast pitch softball with and I would like to catch a couple of innings. My batting career abruptly ended when I injured my rotator cuff trying to lift an eighty pound mutt with beautiful brown eyes over a fence in southwest Detroit on one of my Big Dog rescue missions. I miss playing but still try to support the team. I wonder if Jane will be surprised to see me today.

Jane is the best pitcher in the city of Detroit in the Women's Over Forty Division. People come to the games just to watch her signature pitch, the way she winds up and fires the ball in with the tying run on base. Almost all of the women are lesbian on the team but no one knows for sure about Jane. When her teammates tease her about what a good catch she will make for some lucky woman she only winks and says, "I'm waiting for the right one to come along."

According to Laverne, she might not be waiting too patiently.

I watch for about twenty minutes and Jane doesn't see me in the crowd. It's just as well, things are so strained between us right now, hopefully we will all be back to normal as soon as Ginger and Darilyn are found and the murder is solved.

The noise and general camaraderie of a dozen boisterous relatives will help me stop obsessing over Ginger for a while. After dinner, my uncles sit down at the cleared off dining room table and start their weekly ritual. For the last two years, it's always been Sequence. I can't resist playing a few hands although I can rarely beat them. It's good practice. After playing with them, I can beat almost everyone else.

"Take these leftovers home for your lunch tomorrow," my mother instructs as she fills a recycled grocery bag with several plastic containers. Even with all of the relatives here today, my Mom always has something left over for me. "I packed some extra stew beef for Skipper. Don't forget to bring him next time, Carla." One good thing about Mom; she never knows when something is wrong. Since my father had a stroke last year, all of her attention is on him. When I go into the living room to say good-bye, he looks so used up, like a crumpled empty paper bag sitting slumped in that damn wheel chair.

"Good Night, Da. Hurry up and get better. I need you" As I tenderly kiss his cheek, I think I see a concerned look in his eyes. I wonder if he understands me. I need his advice about so many things. If I could tell him about Ginger, he would know what to do.

Skip is happy to see Mom's beef stew but not so happy when I explain we will not be going out for a walk because it is too late and too dark. I'm tired, but I want to read the weekend editions and compare the information I found on the Internet last night. According to the Free Press, Belinda Norton was the wife of a very wealthy local businessman and the only daughter of the pastor of Detroit's largest Baptist church. The fact that both of the missing women are single and living an alternative lifestyle is at first only peripherally mentioned. A sidebar to the murder investigation story lists as missing Darilyn D'Angelo, the owner of a vegetarian restaurant, and Ginger Harris, a barmaid at Les Girls. I'm relieved that the papers haven't identified Ginger as a member of the Harris family from Grosse Pointe yet. The investigation sells papers, and local radio stations are already picking up the story. By Monday afternoon drive time, the lesbian angle will be making the rounds on talk radio, and civil rights groups will be making angry speeches and getting equal airtime.

Jeremy Norton
Detroit
Tuesday evening, Sept 12, 2000

Alone. So many people the last five days, so many questions. The police at the door Friday morning telling me Belinda is dead. My beautiful Belinda. They ask, "Why don't you know where she was at on Thursday night? Why didn't you wake up when she didn't come home on time? Why didn't you go and look for her? Where were you on Thursday night?"

I ask myself, "Why didn't I tell her how much I loved her? Why did I go to Vegelina's Thursday night to look for her?"

Her mother crying, crying, crying. Her father looking at me with accusing eyes. So many calls to make, the funeral home, the cemetery, the church. So many calls to answer: the police, Belinda's brothers, her friends.

The funeral service at her father's church with tears, questions, sympathy, and underlying it all—silent accusations.

When will it end? Questions, tears, questions. How can I go through this alone, without her?

The big man sits writing for a long time. Two envelopes, one stamp. He puts on his oldest jacket and goes out to the car.

Military personnel are disembarking from troopships this month at
Tan Son Nhut along with an additional 500 helicopters and planes.

—*Newspaper Headline Sept 1, 1966*

BJ Brown
Vietnam
September 1966

I was one of the sixteen thousand Americans off loaded from a giant troopship onto Vietnam soil this month to conquer our enemies. To put that into perspective, the town I was born in and my grandmother still lives in has a population of 4, 596 men, women, and children.

Twelve nurses have arrived in Vietnam with the U.S. 1st Cavalry Division. Four of us are military; the other eight are Red Cross volunteers. The only female Army officer on board ship with us is a nurse returning for her second tour of duty. Recognizing how frightened our small group of nurses is, she intuitively put us at ease by asking us a bit about ourselves and introduced herself as Peggy Ford from Brooklyn. All I could think of to say was, "Only twelve nurses for 16,000 soldiers?" incredulously over and over again. When we all start laughing, it was the first time I had laughed since I found out that Bobby was killed in action. It was my first taste of the macabre humor endemic in all wars.

As soon as we disembarked, the nurses were dispatched to the Chief Nurse's office to be interviewed privately and quickly. I was the only nurse assigned to Qui Nhon. Peggy seemed pleased and told me this was a good assignment and relatively safe. She would be working in the surgical unit in the hospital in Qui Nhon, so we would make the trip together. The other nurses and I said a hurried goodbye and good luck. Nearly two hundred of us were crammed into a C-130 transport plane for the three hour flight to Qui Nhon. It was raining very hard for the entire flight, and we could hear low growls of thunder close by. One of the flight crew said this plane was originally designed to transport supplies. Everyone laughed when the soldier squeezed next to him indiscreetly and loudly joked, "The American government must consider soldiers supplies now because this plane is transporting only live troops today."

Peggy and I were the only females on the plane so we got special treatment. The captain let us ride in the cockpit with the flight crew.

There were fifteen American nurses assigned to Qui Nhon Hospital when I arrived. Four nurses each shared a one story wood frame building. I was hoping for a private room or maybe a big dormitory where there would be lots of people. The thought of sharing a room with one woman unnerved me more than I would have expected. Each building had two rooms and one centrally located bath the four of us were expected to share. There was only one building that had an open bed when I arrived. My roommate had already been chosen for me.

A cute redhead with a big smile and a million freckles was waiting when Peggy and I arrived at the housing units. She grabbed my luggage with one hand while she stuck the other one out for a handshake. "Welcome to Vietnam. I'm Carolyn Stephens and you must be my new roommate. We have been expecting you." I looked at Peggy and she nodded imperceptibly. I tried to grab my bag back, but Carolyn was already headed toward the unit farthest from where the jeep had stopped.

"I'll only be here until June. Then I will be on my way back to Kansas."
I had to hurry to catch up to her. "How long have you been in Qui Nhon? Do you like it here?"

"When my best friend and I went to Kansas City to enlist, the recruiter told me I would never be assigned to a combat zone. I didn't know they were allowed to lie like that. I've been here three months, which is three months too long, but the people at the hospital are nice. I just miss my family and friends so much."

Now I realized it was the smile that made Carolyn cute. Without it, she looked like the plain farm girl she had been before enlisting. I didn't know how to reply. Maybe this really was a safe place to be assigned. Peggy said this was a good assignment. This either backed her up or was part of the BIG LIE. RJ didn't tell any of us what the recruiter in Detroit said to him about being sent to a combat zone.

Peggy and Janice shared the other room in our quarters. When Carolyn showed me our room, I was surprised to find out we all had real beds with good, firm mattresses. The rooms were actually big enough for dressers and a mirror. Carolyn was sympathetic when I opened my suitcase and everything was damp. She offered to find a Hotbox for me to use. They were storage boxes with a light bulb in them used during monsoon season to keep clothes from becoming mildewed. It didn't matter to me because I had already been assigned fatigues, combat boots, and a matching baseball cap for everyday wear. The few things I brought from home had no place here. If I never wore my civvies again, I really didn't care.

Mamma Tuyen, a kind looking middle aged Vietnamese lady, helped me put away my things and hung my damp things on a clothesline she set up outside our quarters. Peggy told me we each paid her two dollars a week, and she did our cleaning, boot shining, and wash. I didn't feel right about this arrangement, but Peggy told me this was a very good salary for her, better than what she could have earned working anywhere else in town.

Carolyn had taken the bed closest to the door. It didn't matter to me till Peggy warned me her bed was on the other side of the plywood wall next to my bed, and I better not snore or talk in my sleep. As everyone laughed, I felt a twinge of homesickness. These three women would be my family, and there were so many secrets I must keep from them.

I was too naïve to realize they were keeping secrets from me too.

Carla McCarthy
Montrose
Monday Morning, Sept. 11, 2000

"Good morning, Pete. You're here early. What's up?" I notice his shirt is more rumpled than usual. I wonder if he has been sleeping in his clothes again.

"I couldn't sleep, so I might as well be here. We got out a Special Edition over the weekend. Ziggy and I had to deliver extra papers to Roseville and the Shores ourselves on Saturday" he gloats. "The 'burbs love a murder mystery when it is not in their backyard."

"What do you need from me today?" I have a serious conflict of interest, but no one seems to notice, or if they do, they don't care.

"I'm working on some editorials. I want our readers to know that The Times agrees with people who say we need to reinforce family values. What was a minister's daughter doing out in the middle of the night, by herself? My mother stayed home every night until I graduated from high school," Pete sputters illogically.

I notice Pete's face is red. I wonder if he is developing high blood pressure from all of his ranting and raving. "Pete, calm down! Belinda Norton didn't have any children, and we don't know what happened. Let's not blame the victim."

"Yeah, you're right as usual, McCarthy" Pete relents and lets out a noisy sigh as he tries to get himself under control. "Why don't you write something about the police investigation? The murdered woman's husband, where was he Thursday night? How many other unsolved murders have been committed in Detroit recently?"

"Actually, Pete, I've been working on an article this weekend about how the fear of crime is affecting business in the area. I'm not too keen on the Candid Times pushing the editorial opinion that there may be a serial killer stalking women in Montrose."

"Get over it, McCarthy! We are in business to sell papers, not hand hold a bunch of nervous old ladies." Pete's bad temper is not worth dealing with today so I just walk away.

During the early morning, I spend a couple of hours at my desk using the phone to track down Darilyn and Belinda's past employers, friends, relatives, schoolmates, anyone who might be able to help me make a connection between the two women. Belinda was well known in the Detroit area and many people are willing to talk to me in the hopes it will be helpful in locating her killer. Others just want to be sure I spelled their names right if I quote them.

Belinda Norton was the only daughter of a well-known pastor of one of Detroit's largest Southern Baptist congregations. Her mother was a seamstress who worked at home and raised three children. Belinda attended an all-girls Christian boarding school from the age of eight until her graduation at seventeen. She attended Wayne State University for four years and obtained a Bachelor of Arts degree in Women's Studies. Her older brother Kenneth attended medical school and is practicing obstetrics, and her younger brother Maurice is following their father's path to fame and attending the seminary in St Louis.

Her marriage to Jeremy Norton was at the Detroit Yacht Club on Belle Isle in 1991. She was twenty-one when she married the forty-two year old widower. His first wife had died in childbirth, and he spent the next dozen years amassing a fortune in the used auto sales business.

She was a large contributor to NOW, Planned Parenthood, Democrats for Social Justice and the ACLU and was a member of the American Association of University Women (AAUW). Recently she had taken on a volunteer assignment with Big Sisters. When I call the local chapter of the ACLU, a chatty woman says she knew Belinda but if I wanted to know anything personal about her, I should call Nikki Applegate in San Francisco. I make a note of the name but it doesn't seem necessary to pursue one more friend.

When I finish my calls and break for lunch, I can write an obituary about her but I am not any closer to knowing who killed her or why.

❦   ❦   ❦

It's a quick drive to the Broadway Deli, and I want to see my favorite wait-ress, Nadia. She's busy but when she sees me come in, she smiles, and points to a booth in her section. When she brings my water, there is a slice of lemon in it that I never have to ask for and she only says, "Your usual?" If she doesn't see me for a month, she still remembers what I want. They make an excellent Tur-key Rueben here and instead of fries I can get a side of cottage cheese. Nadia is going to Wayne Community College and raising a three-year-old daughter by herself. After a crummy start in life, I am sure she is going to be successful in whatever she does from now on. I can see she is too busy with the lunch crowd to talk, but when she brings my check, she asks me if I can come back later to talk about something. I wonder if she knows something or just wants reassur-ance that she is safe. She usually only works the lunch shift so she shouldn't be worried about walking to her car. Somehow, I don't think Nadia is the timo-rous type, so it must be something else she needs to talk to me about.

When I get back to my desk, I start making phone calls to London and Van-couver. The information about Darilyn D'Angelo is not as easy to get nor is it as straightforward as what I found out about Belinda Norton.

Darilyn D'Angelo was born to Louisa and Frank Palmeri in Chicago. Her name at birth was Marilyn Palmeri. Her father was a wealthy businessman, well known in the import coffee business. Her mother and father were killed in an automobile accident when Marilyn was nine. Her maternal grandmother was made her guardian, and by mutual consent, she continued her education at St Cecelia's, a private school for girls. After graduating from high school with honors, she attended a well-respected Catholic college known for its dis-tinguished international curriculum. The college was annually ranked as one of the top ten liberal arts colleges in the Midwest. I spoke on the phone with Sister Fernanda who said she remembered Marilyn and seemed to recall a hope she would join their order after college.

At twenty-one, she inherited a modest sum of money from her parents' insurance. It was at this point that she legally changed her name. There was no record of her marrying. Her family's considerable estate would come to her when she turned thirty or to her husband if she were married. She used the insurance money to go to France where she studied in Provence for three years and then worked in highly acclaimed restaurants in London, Berlin, and Amsterdam. She formed a pattern of never working more than a year or two in each country.

After that she seemed to have dropped out of sight for two years before returning to North America to work at a four star restaurant in Vancouver. True to the style she had perfected in Europe, she didn't stay long in Canada either.

She returned to the US and opened Vegelina's in Montrose about six months ago. She told the realtor who found the vacant building for her that she was tired of traveling and wanted to settle down in a pleasant small town, close to a big city. She said she had paid her dues and was ready to own her own restaurant and be her own boss for the first time in her life.

At what is becoming our usual table at Maria's Monday evening the police chief and I compare notes. She is preparing a P.O.P., Predicted Offender Profile, by comparing profiles of the three women. I am mildly surprised when she confides that Ginger has a criminal record and very surprised when she adds that her arrest was for a violent offence. I know better than to ask anything more about it. Nan, at the moment, is in her official capacity as Chief of Police investigating three possible homicides. She will tell me what I need to know to help her investigation but she will not tell me anything just to satisfy my curiosity.

Name	D. D'Angelo	Belinda Norton	Ginger Harris
Age	34	30	42
Gender	F	F	F
Marital Status	S	M	S
Circumstances	Missing	Dead	Missing
Occupation	Rest. Owner	N/A	Barmaid
Criminal Record	No	No	Yes

Violent Offence			Yes
Sex Offence			No
Drug Offence			No
Ethnicity	White	Black	White

While we are eating, she asks me to tell her what I have found out about Darilyn and Belinda.

"Everything I found on the web is public record. The detectives on the case will already have the facts in both Belinda's and Darilyn's files" I tell Nan. "I did talk to a lot of people and found out some interesting things, though." I fill her in on everything I found out and turn over my notes without her having to ask. The originals are on my desk at home.

"It was around the time she turned thirty that Darilyn dropped out of sight for two years. That coincides with the time she told people in Vancouver that she was in Africa studying a secret women's society."

Nan asks me to hold it a minute while she speed dials some lucky person on her cell phone. I guess when you are the Chief; you can make calls to your subordinates at nine o'clock at night and expect to get a civil answer. "Mike will get back to me on her passport records."

Nan appears very interested when I mention the secret society and starts to ask me something when her damn cell phone ringing interrupts us. She doesn't bother to set it to vibrate when she is in uniform. After a very assertive "Chief Lawson speaking," she listens for a long minute before she disappears out the back door. It is ten minutes before she comes back. I have paid the check and am waiting with my sweater on.

"You're ready? Good, let's go. I need to talk to you"

She doesn't say anything as we drive back to my house five blocks away. I am more puzzled than nervous, but I know something is wrong.

❦   ❦   ❦

"Why didn't you tell me Maria threatened Darilyn Thursday night?" Nan demands as soon as we are in the house. "That was your friend Abigail Carr on the phone. She saw Darilyn's and Ginger's photos in the paper connected with Belinda's murder. The picture must have jogged her memory and she called to fill me in on the night the two of you had dinner at Vegelina's. Tell me what happened and don't leave anything out this time."

I tell her everything including the fact that Maria had been drinking and it was just her usual bluster that never really meant anything. Nan asks me so many questions I start to think she suspects me of something. I'm not sure if I should mention the fact that Darilyn served Abigail and me some wine.

"Look, Nan, I don't know if you know this, or even if you care," I offered, "but sometimes Darilyn will offer her regular customers a little home made Italian wine. She said it was an old family recipe and she kept a little in the kitchen for cooking."

I keep my head down looking at her soft, kid leather, lace up oxfords. Damn, she looks good. I love a woman who wears kick ass shoes.

When she leaves after assuring me that she doesn't give a damn about the wine and also assuring me I am not in trouble with her, I check my voice mail. Abigail Carr had not returned any of my calls.

On my way to bed, I remember Nadia wanted to talk to me after the lunch rush. It's way too late for me to call her now and probably not important. I need to sleep to let my brain sort out this hodgepodge of information.

It feels good to be in bed as I kick off my shoes and put Paisley Park on. I'm still a little hungry so I get an apple to munch. Skip is glad I'm home but he can't figure out why we have eliminated our before bedtime walk.

I toss and turn all the way through Prince and when even Van Morrison doesn't put me to sleep; I decide I may as well get up. My conscience is gnawing at me with tiny little rat-sharp teeth. I know I haven't faced the fact that Ginger might be dead, and I also know I can't sleep while she might need me. Denial is losing steam.

Five hundred US Air Force planes bomb targets in North Vietnam in the heaviest air raid of the war.

—Newspaper Headline September 17

BJ Brown
Vietnam
September 1966

The first few weeks in Vietnam were not what I had prepared myself for. I had expected to be working right on the battlefield in a dripping, fusty tent with bullet holes for ventilation. Luckily, the provincial hospital in Qui Nhon was one of the first the US had updated with standard surgical suites. It consisted of two operating theatres, a six-bed recovery ward, and a central supply unit. It was on the edge of the small town with more than a dozen units of military housing near by.

Behind the hospital, there was a big hill with a beautiful view of the town and the water. We could smell the South China Sea a mile away when there was a breeze. Whenever I had time for a quick break, I would walk up the hill and watch the fishing boats dock. The signal corps had a location on the hill, and it is from there that the Qui Nhon Armed Forces programs were televised. The schedule for all medical personnel was twelve hours on and twelve off with one day off each week. It was hard for me to get used to the rotating day and night shifts at first. Carolyn and I worked days together during my first week. My adrenaline was so high that I couldn't go to sleep at night. The weeks that I was scheduled for days, I usually went back to the hospital to work with Peggy and Janice after dinner. I could eat in the mess hall at the hospital; I didn't need to waste the time going out. Training in the emergency wards in Detroit had not prepared me for shrapnel wounds and mortar burns that were my everyday cases here. Every day, casualties poured in as if there were continuous train wrecks, bombings, and deadly fires all happening outside my door at the same time.

On my first day off, I sat in the sunny courtyard trying to read. Hoping it would hold my attention, I picked up a new Jacqueline Susann paperback. I was surprised to find a supply of American paperbacks and current magazines at the PX right there on the hospital grounds. It was over 80 degrees and we are coming out of the monsoon season, so I was hoping it wouldn't rain that day.

Peggy told me the weather should be warm and dry until about Easter. I noticed Carolyn coming out of our rooms with her swim suit on. The smell of tanning lotion reached me before I could hear what she was saying.

"Let's go to the beach! It's a perfect day," Carolyn coaxed. "A swim is exactly what we need today."

"I offered to work today but the Captain refused. He told me I'll need this day of rest soon enough," I replied, anxious to get back to my book.

"You can rest on the beach," Carolyn insisted. "I don't want to go alone."

It was hard to argue with a woman in a bathing suit. I put my swimsuit on under my fatigues and walked the mile to the beach with her. It was easier than I expected to make "getting to know you" small talk with her.

"It was so damned hot last summer in Michigan, so far Vietnam is cooler than I expected," I offered, feeling safe with the weather.

"It's a lot like Florida where my grandmother lives," Carolyn said happily, and with grandmothers to talk about, we found we had something in common.

When we arrived at the water less than twenty minutes later, I left my fatigues neatly folded on the pearly sand beach and waded into the water. It felt good to be floating in the azure sea looking up at the brilliant blue cloudless sky, and for awhile that afternoon, I was carefree.

That night I dreamed I was swimming in a fast moving river and the current was very strong. I could see Bobby in his swimsuit playing on the banks of the river. Two grown-ups in black clothes lifted him up by his skinny little arms and put him in a strange looking foreign car. I was terrified when I realized it was the Rosenbergs. Somehow, they had escaped execution and they were going to punish Bobby for what Daddy said about them. I swam and I swam but I couldn't get back to shore.

After that, I didn't want to swim any more. Vietnam was not a place for the dreams of Barbara Jane Brown.

I learned to exist in two worlds during that time in Vietnam. Each world was defined by the sounds inhabiting it. The traditional boundaries between day and night had lost their meaning. At first, bomb blasts were only a distant drone, merely background sounds. I learned to ignore them, much as I had learned fifteen years ago to ignore the pervasive hum of V6 engines and the angry buzz of muscle cars when I was transplanted from farmland to the Motor City. They no longer interrupted my sleep.

A change came when a series of intense battles at Dak To brought a constant stream of severe casualties from the field. A continual shriek from the medics' sirens announced the arrival of injured and dying men. It became impossible for me to sleep when enemy soldiers nightly dropped shells and mortars closer to us. Battle noises surrounding the hospital were horrific and I could no longer deny the world of war I lived in.

There were only brief glimpses of the other world. Some nights from the top of the hill behind the hospital, we could hear little groups of American personnel sitting outside their quarters in the valley singing familiar, sad love songs. Every Sunday night a few of the doctors and nurses got together and spent an hour or so singing hymns. One medic in particular, I never knew who it was, had a great romantic baritone voice. He sounded a bit like Elvis Presley when he sang "Are You Lonesome Tonight?"

Carla McCarthy
Montrose
Tuesday Morning Sept 12, 2000

The Candid Times prints a Special Edition Tuesday morning with Belinda Norton's photo next to Ginger and Darilyn's. The headline shouts MUR-DERED in bold capital letters. If you didn't read carefully, you would assume three bodies had been found. I know better, but looking at those pictures side by side like that has me spooked. What could the three women have had in common? I wonder if the fact that they were women who were alone on Thursday night could be enough of a reason. Could it have been me as I walked to my car alone that night? I feel a little extra warm, fuzzy feeling for my old friend Nan. She is always around when I need her. When this is over, I am going to take her to a Bed and Breakfast on Pelee Island. No one will recognize her on the Canadian Island and she can relax for a couple of days. I will show her how much I appreciate her.

Pete has the pictures I took which will prove Belinda was at Laverne and Shirley's Thursday night. Based on her reactions to my photo taking, she didn't want anyone to know it. No one seemed to know where Ginger was, and I saw Darilyn at her own restaurant a block away. Is there a connection?

I find a box of doughnut holes someone has left on Pete's desk. What a bunch of suck-ups around here, I think. While I drink a barely warm coffee from Tim Horton's and finish the doughnuts, I use a legal size pad of yellow paper and drew a diagram of both sides of the 9 Mile Road in downtown Montrose.

One of the things that have everyone puzzled is why all of the women's cars were still in the parking lots Friday morning. It was as if someone had just beamed the women up. Darilyn's new yellow convertible was in the parking lot next to Belinda's car. Both cars stayed there for two days until the cops towed them in. Ginger's car was in the large parking lot on the other side of the street behind China Jane's and the Hair Boutique.

I am trying to think logically about this and keep my thoughts from rushing ahead. It feels like I am on to some gigantic discovery if I can just put together what happened.

If Ginger and Darilyn got in a car with someone else, did they do it willingly? If so, who was it and why haven't they contacted someone? If they didn't go willingly, what has happened to them?

By this time, I am tired of playing the IF Game. My reporter's instinct tell me I am close to some answers, but I am going to have to go back to the parking lot and visualize the possibilities for myself.

I give Pete a courtesy call to tell him I am on my way to 9 Mile Rd. to check on a hunch. Against my gut instincts, I tell him to see what he can turn up on Laverne and Shirley. He wants to know if I am onto something, but I'm not sure where my hunch is going to lead me, so I just ask him to check the basics. Who owned the businesses on 9 Mile Rd., how long had they been in business, any BBB complaints, any criminal records?

By the time I get to the parking lot, it is lunch time. Cars are coming and going, quickly picking up take out orders from China Jane's. Other cars are parking for short trips to Drug Mart or the cleaners on Woodward Ave. The September sun at high noon is benign but warm enough for people to linger a little on their lunch time errands. When I pull up across from the trio of businesses, I have a little time to think while I am waiting for the parking spot I want. One business is a restaurant owned by a single woman. The next is a hair salon owned by a single woman, and the third is a bookstore jointly owned by two women. All of the women are about the same age but with very different backgrounds. I realize that I know very little about Jane's past and even less about Tootsie's.

I put the kill switch on before I leave the DeSoto, put two quarters in the meter, and walk a straight path across the street to Tootsie's back door. No twinkling Christmas lights greet me today. Tootsie's back door is vibrantly painted in a rainbow design with several sets of realistic looking eyes in various shapes and hues peeking out between cloud shapes and at the end of the rainbow. By contrast, the institutional white back door to the Chinese restaurant is a little dingy with hand prints from customers coming and going with hands full of paper sacks filled with fried rice and moon cakes. The two businesses are actually in the same concrete block building divided by plaster walls. A plain door inserted between the two stores is padlocked and appears to lead nowhere. There clearly is not enough room for another business there.

My cell phone is ringing and I recognize the number as someone from the Times. "I've got all of the information you asked for this morning," our new intern is boasting.

Pete hired an intern, a journalism major from Wayne State, to help with research. With weekend special editions, Pete can use the help. It's good to see Pete getting involved. He is reacting to this story with more interest than I have seen from him in a long time.

"Thanks, I know I didn't ask for this specifically, but did you by chance come up with a blue print or some kind of schematic for the stores along here? I need to know why there is a door between the Chinese restaurant and the hair salon. This building has been remodeled several times since it was built, and the door is probably just a remnant from another incarnation, but I'm curious why there is a padlock on it."

"I'll leave this other stuff on your desk for you, Ms McCarthy, and go to work on that," he promises eagerly. I've noticed Pete does not hire female interns any more.

I head for the Deli to see if Nadia still wants to talk to me. She's busy working the lunch crowd as I suspected but still she looks glad to see me. "I'm sorry I didn't get back yesterday. Things are kind of crazy right now," I start out but she is shaking her head impatient with my excuses. "Doesn't matter. I need to tell you something about Darilyn. It might be important."

Nadia asks her boss for a five minute break. When we step outside, I listen in utter amazement to a condensed version of the story of her relationship with Darilyn. When she hurries back into the restaurant, I speed dial Nan and tell her what Nadia has told me.

While I'm waiting for the Chief, Nadia brings an order of cottage cheese, a turkey Rueben, and an iced tea. I'm sitting in a booth near the back door at the Broadway where I can watch the parking lot. My phone is flashing with missed calls on my voice mail. The first is a message from my sister reminding me we are supposed to eat at her house on Sunday. The second is from Leesa. She is on her way to Michigan and she wants me to pick her up at the airport tonight at seven thirty.

I hope whatever she has to tell me about Darilyn is worth it.

BJ's Letters Home
Vietnam
1966–1967

November 11, 1966
Qui Nhon

Hi Patti,

Surprise! Me writing a letter! How are you and everybody in Detroit? Everything is okay here. Thanks for all of the cards and letters. I just haven't had time to write. Getting settled in here has been weird. We work twelve hour days and at least six days a week. It's not all work, though. You would be amazed at how many parties there are. Everyone from the doctors and nurses to the ambulance drivers and the maintenance staff get together to party whenever there is a free night (which isn't too often lately). It seems like most of the Americans here drink heavily and a lot of them use drugs too. Not that I blame them.

It's been warm and dry since I've been here. The three months seem like three years in some ways. I went swimming in the South China Sea! A long way from Belle Isle and the Detroit River! In May the Monsoon season starts and it will rain every day, so I may as well enjoy it while I can.

I live and work with three other American nurses. We share a two bedroom house. Carolyn is my roommate. She is from Kansas and hates it here. She can't wait to go home when her tour of duty is over in June. She is very nice but insipid, if you know what I mean. Boring! Our room always smells like the coconut oil she slathers on every day so she will tan. With her red hair, I doubt she would tan if she stayed here until the war is over.

My other roommates are Peggy and Janice. Peggy is the head nurse at the hospital and technically my boss. She reports directly to the Nursing Director. She and Janice share the other room and they seem to be very close friends. I think Peggy signed on for a second tour of duty just to stay with Janice.

You've asked me what the working conditions are like here. Well, first of all, more combat troops keep arriving every month. Casualties arrive at the hospital by helicopter, but depending on where the battles are, they might be brought in on a stretcher carried by other soldiers or in a Medic van that has traveled a hundred miles to get here. Sometimes, the vans arrive with bullet holes in them! By the time the patients get here, they are often in wretched condition.

Carolyn and I work in Emergency and Receiving doing triage. That is so difficult, Patty. It is not like the hospitals in Detroit where we were sorting heart attacks from pneumonia. The injuries I see most often are gunshot wounds, napalm burns (nasty), head injuries, and fractures.

Peggy assists in the Surgery Unit and the doctors often operate all night long. Janice cares for the patients post-op and I think her job is the hardest. She is the one who has to care for soldiers when they wake up and their arms or legs have been amputated. That is hard on all of us.

A nice Vietnamese woman takes care of us. I like her a lot. Sometimes we go for a walk together after dinner. Well, it's time for me to go back to work. Tell your brother I said hi.

Bye for now,

BJ

February 14, 1967

Hi Grandma,

Happy Valentine's Day! Thanks for the card, I got it yesterday. The mail here is surprisingly good. Could you mail me some oatmeal cookies? Just kidding. Actually the food is good here too, just not as good as your home cooking. The Vietnamese lady who takes care of our housing unit (her name is Mama Tuyen) introduced me to her oldest brother, Vo Manh Lanh. He is a baker. He makes durian mooncakes, honey biscuits, doughnuts, coffeecakes, and even apple pies. He is learning to speak English and likes to talk to me to practice. His dream is to move to America and run his own restaurant. I trade him American magazines from the PX for mooncakes and honey biscuits that I can share with the other nurses at the hospital.

I guess you will be starting your vegetable garden in a couple of weeks. I would love to have some of those tomatoes and green onions. We tried to grow those in Michigan but they just weren't as good as yours.

To answer your questions: No, of course I have not started smoking. I promised you I wouldn't and you know I keep my promises. Yes, I still drink coffee but I have no idea how much it costs. Maybe you should try growing coffee beans if it is getting so expensive. With your green thumb, you could have the first coffee plantation in Missouri!

We have many kinds of birds here. I wish you could be here just for one day to see them. They are so different from the Blue Jays and Cardinals we had in Michigan. The most common birds in this part of the country are Blue Rumped Pittas and Collared Laughingthrushes! Too funny! You might think I am making up these names just to amuse you but I'm not. Well if you can write to me about Minnie the Moocher, I will write to you about Pitta and her blue rump!

Take care of yourself and Minnie, your friend the mooching crow. I will be home before you know it and I am coming straight to your house. We will sit on the front porch and rock ourselves to sleep every night.

Love,
Barbara Jane

April 1, 1967

Hi Mama,

Thanks for the Care package and the letters. How are you doing? I hope the pills Dr. Hudson gave you are helping and you are sleeping better. Things are okay here. Lately I've been having bad dreams. I had dinner with Tuyen and her niece, Vo Thi Ly, last night. Tuyen means Angel. I am getting used to the names. Ly (pronounced Lee) works in a clothing shop in Qui Nhon. I bought some silk material there and ordered a Vietnamese suit. It has a long red jacket and loose white pants. Very exotic, maybe I can wear it on New Year's Eve. Let me know if you want anything made. Nice material is very cheap here.

It's about a mile and a half to the center of town from where I work. The streets are narrow and crowded with a lot of military trucks and jeeps. The only cars for civilian use are actually little carts called Lambreetas. Don't tell Dad. He will want to buy one! Women and old men all ride bicycles. I'd like to have my old Schwinn here to ride back and forth to town.

Everything seems very dusty right now but the monsoons will start soon and everything will turn to mud. Mothers here don't worry about baby sitters. Kids and dogs, both covered with flies are on every corner but they seem happy enough. I guess the dogs keep the kids out of the streets. Babies and toddlers are all naked from the waist down, which I thought was very bizarre until I realized there are no such things as diapers here.

Peggy and Janice want to update our quarters before the monsoons come in June. Even though Carolyn is scheduled to leave in June, she is always willing to go along with anything Peggy wants to do. I guess the majority rules because all winter we've been working on making our tidy little quarters less sterile looking. Janice miraculously came up with some robin's egg blue paint and some white knotted cotton to make curtains with. We are lucky. American women can get pretty much whatever we ask for in Qui Nhon.

We are all going to celebrate our revamped quarters with a little house-warming party at our place with some of the medics from the base and the other nurses from the hospital.

Today is my day off but I am going over to the clinic as soon as I finish this. I am working as many hours as I can. It just feels like the right thing to do.

Tell Daddy and everyone hello,

Barbara Jane

May 1, 1967

Dear Patty,

Big party tonight and I drank too much. Some of those GIs really get to me. They are always saying I look like their sister or their girlfriend. I never want to be anybody's sister or girlfriend ever again. Did I ever tell you that everybody here calls me BJ? Yep, I changed my name when I was in Basic Training.

I've been having these crazy dreams that RJ is not really dead, maybe he is just missing in action. Maybe he will be brought into the OR and I will be the one to save him. Maybe he will forgive me if he knows what a good nurse I am. Maybe if he had a nurse like me after he was ambushed he would still be alive.

Patty, you have been a good friend. I probably won't mail this but if I do, please don't tell me again that RJ's death is not my fault. I know it is. I am trying to make up for it, though.

Your friend,

BJ Brown

June 15, 1967

Hi Grandma,

Do you know I saved all of your letters since 1953 when we moved to Michigan? Let's see, one a month for 14 years, that's a lot! Someday, I am going to put them all together and make a book. I'll bet not too many people know as much about crows as you do. Ha Ha

My roommates are all very nice girls and I am surprised what good friends we are becoming. When I first got here, I was afraid we wouldn't get along. Peggy is from New York, Carolyn is from Kansas City (not too far from you), and Janice is from Milwaukee. We are all so different but it doesn't seem to matter as much as it did at first.

Last week Janice let it slip that it was her birthday. I made a rushed trip into town (I needed my bike) and had Lanh (Tuyen's brother) make a chocolate cake as a surprise for her. We surprised her in the mess hall and everyone sang Happy Birthday while she blew out the candles. Oh, I did ask Lanh for his recipe for durian moon cakes. Do we have durians in the US? It is some kind of fruit (like plums mixed with bananas). We are trying to get it translated into English and I will mail it to you. He said you could make it with other fruit if you can't find durians.

Carolyn's one-year tour of duty is up this month and she is scheduled to go to Germany in two weeks. She can't wait to leave. I'll miss her more than I thought. She and I have been teaching Ly and Lanh American folk songs. She is the only one here who knew "Sixteen Tons."

I am going to volunteer for a special program helping civilians. It is not dangerous. Don't worry. I'll tell you about it after I start.

Love,
Barbara Jane

July 1, 1967

Hi Pat,

Sure, you can change your name too. I will try to call you Pat if you will remember to call me BJ. Pat does sound more grown up than Patty. Now that you are 21, you can drink, vote, and call yourself Pat!

Well, the infamous monsoons are here. They have taken charge. The rains are torrential and constant. Remember how much I always enjoyed thunder and lightning at home? How many times did we walk in the rain just for the heck of it? The rain is different here. It sounds like a macabre symphony with thunder and lightning in harmony with assault rifles and bomb blasts.

I try not to talk about bombs and guns and I notice no one else does either. I am getting more and more frustrated and angry every day. Maybe it is the rain, maybe it is the lack of sleep. Peggy (my boss) noticed my edginess and suggested I might like to volunteer for Madcap, the Medical Civilian Aid Program. She thinks the experience will be good for me, and it will give me something productive to do with my off duty hours.

I've told the Nursing Director to send me wherever she needs me. Medical teams go out every week to orphanages, the Leprosarium, and a dozen refugee camps. I will have my first assignment at a refugee camp next week, so you may not hear from me for a little while.

Take care,

BJ

PS: DON'T ENLIST

Carla McCarthy
Montrose
Tuesday late afternoon, Sept 12, 2000

The Hair Boutique is a very strange but wonderful place. If it were in Spain, Anton Gaudi could have designed it. Mardi Gras style beads in every color cover the walls and drape seductively over various sized gaudily framed mirrors. Plastic and silk flowers bloom all year long and client and celebrity photos are pinned haphazardly to a corkboard. Velcro hair rollers in various sizes and colors have been fashioned to represent human and animal figures in a variety of improbable poses.

At least two dozen dolls wearing a variety of wigs inhabit the place. The dolls are sitting on shampoo sinks, hanging on the coat rack, piled together on swivel chairs, and one pair is peeking out from behind the cash register. There are flaming Lucille Ball reds, glamorous Marilyn Monroe platinum blondes, and Elizabeth Taylor Cleopatra Queen of the Nile black. It can be quite disconcerting to use the john here, I've been told. Tootsie wears whichever wig fits her mood while she is working or schmoozing with friends or clients.

Tootsie signals friends and customers that she is in residence by turning on a long string of miniature white Christmas lights in the front windows. I have never dared go in for a hair cut or even a manicure. I have seen clients leaving but somehow I know they have a different idea of feminine grooming than I do.

Tootsie Siegel is as outgoing and vivacious as her next door neighbor China Jane is taciturn and reserved. She seems genuinely pleased to see me and enthusiastically hugs me as though we are old friends. It's as though she has completely forgotten our last encounter about the McGuire twins at Jane's. I have seen her a few times around the 'hood but we have never had a conversation. If I didn't know better, I would think she tries to avoid me. When she gives me the evil eye, I figure it may be because I never come in for a hair cut. Surely, she can take a look at me and see I am more the Fantastic Sam's type. When I get there a little before six she must have just opened because there are no customers waiting for her, and she is polishing her nails a bright red to match her Lucille Ball 1950's hair style today. The radio is tuned to an oldies station that plays music from the fifties and sixties exclusively. It's impossible to tell how old she is because she wears so much make up. As we are talking, I notice she is mouthing the words from the songs and probably wishing I would leave or at least stop talking so she could belt out those famous Bill Haley words:

"One, two, three o'clock, four o'clock rock, we're going to rock around the clock tonight! We're going to rock, rock, rock till broad day light. When the clock strikes four, we'll yell for more. We're going to rock around the clock tonight!"

I ask her if she has heard anything about Darilyn or Ginger or if she can think of anything that might give us a clue if they are together. I'm sorry I asked as soon as she starts telling me every rumor and opinion that has been expressed by every one of her gossipy and highly imaginative clients this week.

"Ginger and Darilyn are mother and daughter and when they were reunited they left the country together to look for Darilyn's father. He's a fugitive from the FBI and hiding out in Switzerland" was a story straight from everyone's favorite soap opera. Others thought they were clandestine lovers who hooked up during the black out in August when Montrose lost power due to a downed electrical grid during the height of the summer heat. That story had Ginger eating tofu calzones at Vegelina's when the lights went out and they had fallen in love by the time the air conditioning came back on two and a half days later. They kept their relationship a secret so Ginger could continue her lucrative career. As an unattached barmaid, she would naturally make better tips than if her devoted customers knew she was planning on eloping with Darilyn as soon as they saved enough money to go to Canada to get married."

On and on she goes and I try to pay attention, but the stories seem so ludicrous and I am so tired, it is hard to concentrate. I am watching her as she keeps talking, when I start to imagine she is Pete's mother in drag. I want to laugh out loud, but I am afraid she will think I am laughing at the story she is telling me. There is an incredible resemblance hidden behind the big hair and the make-up. The women are the same height and size and both have nice brown eyes.

I wonder if this could be Pete's aunt who bought a house in Montrose last year. No wonder he has not brought her into the office to introduce her. What a character! I'll have to ask him about her one day, if I can ever catch him in a good mood.

Trying to bring the conversation back to reality, I ask her if she realizes that the murdered woman found in Vegelina's was right next door at Laverne and Shirley's the night she was murdered. She looks totally bewildered at this news.

"Next door? What was she doing next door? Nobody told us she was next door. It could have been me that was murdered! Shirley has a terrible temper. I hope she didn't do it."

I think I should change the subject. "What about the cars? Why do you think all of their cars were left in the metered parking lots?"

That brings her up short. "I'm sure I don't know. Why would you ask me a question like that? I am not under suspicion, am I? I didn't even know Darilyn left her car behind the restaurant. I hardly even know Darilyn, why are you asking me about her? I thought you were just worried about Ginger or I would never have talked to you. This is not fair." Tootsie looks like she is ready to cry. I can't handle another crying woman today.

Whew! What brought that on? I am not well equipped for tears. Picking up my sweater and camera bag, I edge slowly towards the door. Her tears and bewilderment quickly turn to anger when she sees I am leaving. "Oh, go on! Go back to the Candid Times and tell them all about it. Pete will believe anything you say."

More puzzled than ever, I decide to head home, feed Skip, and the cats before I head for the airport to pick up Leesa. My car doesn't have a CD player and I distrust the radio for a ride longer than thirty minutes, so I pick up some portable headphones and Purple Rain and head for Metro Airport.

BJ Brown
Vietnam
August, 1967

Refugee camps in South Vietnam were overflowing with young women and small children. Women with babies in their arms fled their family huts and came to the refuge camp because they feared for the lives of their children. The only things they could talk about were their farms being bombed and the deaths of their families. At first, I adamantly blamed the Viet Cong for their situation, but I slowly began to realize it was just as often American bombs destroying the countryside farms and homes.

A few displaced Catholic families left their homes in North Vietnam because of the Communists. They came to the camps but did not stay very long. Anyone who had any money or who could still earn money would end up in Saigon where the conditions were a little better.

The living conditions were horribly over crowded for everyone in the camps. Week by week, the refugee camps grew, in what seemed like over night, from three hundred refugees in each camp to three thousand or more villagers of all ages. The skimpy food supply was rationed, but black market activity determined who ate. Many of the old people and women were suffering from malnutrition. They gave their shares of food to the men in their families who had to fight or to the babies and children.

Tin huts provided the only shelter and there were not enough latrines. Unsanitary conditions were made worse by a lack of clean water. Five husky Marine volunteers spent their weekend off building cement block buildings for latrines. By Tuesday, the refugees had found a way to lock the buildings and used them for rice storage. They didn't share our need for privacy but keeping their food safe was of paramount importance to them.

The training I had at Ft. Sam Houston paid off when we set up open air clinics in the middle of the camps. The stench and the heat were a little more bearable if we could get a breeze. During the four hours we were at a camp each week, we treated civilians for eye infections, diarrhea, worms, and a variety of skin problems. People who were healthy before the war were susceptible to many illnesses that could have been avoided easily with basic hygiene and a nutritional food supply. Many of the young women and children standing in line were not actually sick but they needed vitamins and hygiene supplies. Mark, a young dentist from New Jersey, set up his portable chair on the edge of the clinic just to pull rotten teeth. I was amazed to see he always had a long line although every patient under ten left crying.

A common complaint was what we euphemistically called "The Crud." We treated it the same way we treated infected insect bites. If it looked particularly virulent, we gave them an antibiotic salve and told them how to apply it. That was one time we did not feel bad about not being more "hands on" with their treatment.

Out of the three hundred patients we saw during our weekly visit, some of the cases were more serious. Each week I saw patients with tuberculosis, many that had gone untreated for years. I felt good to know the medicine we gave them helped. Occasionally a leper would show up at the clinic. We had medicines that could stop the spread of leprosy, but there was no help for the damage that had already been done to their body.

A translator traveled with us but I tried to communicate with my patients directly. I would point to myself and say BEE JAY. I often would say "Qui Nhon" and many of them seemed to know there was a hospital there. Some of the older men and women wanted to know if I knew Mama Tuyen. She was a legend in the province for her big family and bigger heart. I was popular and each week the lines grew longer to see the American nurse.

The weeks I went to the orphanages might have been the hardest. The children were so trusting and good natured; it broke my heart to see their many problems. Many of the children were very attractive but already their teeth were rotting. The sugar cane fields that supported their families provided an irresistible treat to the children. Mothers gave their teething toddlers a piece to chew to quiet them and the older children chewed it routinely. By the time their permanent teeth were coming in, they were already rotted, and the children were lining up for the dentist chair.

When we drove up to the orphanages, the children would run shrieking out to meet us. We brought clothing, food, and even some small toys for them as well as medicine and vaccines. Our medic trucks, which somehow got the nickname Cracker Boxes, with the big red crosses on the doors, were a symbol, a harbinger of hope.

Before my year was up, I had already decided I would ask for another year in country with a new assignment. I didn't want to be so close to anyone. I had heard rumors about a tough assignment that no one wanted. A place called CuChi.

Carla McCarthy
Montrose
Tuesday Evening, Sept 12, 2000

Leesa and I are back at my house by 8:30. Nan answers right away when I call her private number, and says she will be over in a few minutes. While Leesa and Skip are renewing their friendship, I make a pot of green tea for us. It looks like she is planning to stay with me while she is in town. At least she didn't bring any serious luggage, just a small over night bag. She looks better than I remember her.

"The clean Canadian air agrees with you, Leesa."

"Thanks," she smiles. "But you see I've gained some weight since the last time I saw you."

"You must have stopped eating brown rice and organic seaweed. It's hard to gain weight on that." I hope I don't sound churlish, but if anyone could gain weight on that, it would be me.

When we were in college together, she was on some weird macrobiotic diet. She has gained a little weight, which looks good on her.

We make small talk easily enough, but when she starts to talk about Darilyn and what happened in Vancouver, I ask her to wait until Nan gets here. The chief is going to want to hear it all and I doubt if I want to hear it twice.

"I'm a little anxious about talking to the police," she admits. It hasn't occurred to me that Leesa might be nervous about talking to the Chief of Police.

"Nan is an old friend of mine and just wants to find out what is happening to the women in her community," I reassure her. I know Leesa would feel better about it if she knew Nan was a lesbian, but I don't think it is right for me to tell her. I emphasize the "old friend" part, hoping she won't think "old friend" is the current euphemism for ex girl-friend. I wonder how long it will take her to guess when she meets her.

Nan rings the bell before nine o'clock, and when I open the door, the waitress from the Broadway Deli is right behind her. Nadia is saying, "I hope you don't mind," while Nan is making herself at home introducing herself to Leesa and setting up her tape recorder. I am surprised Nan is not in uniform tonight. The snug fitting dark brown gabardine slacks and light blue and white striped cotton shirt are very flattering. The coral v-neck sweater brings out the gray in her blue eyes in a way her uniform never could. I am a little disappointed when I realize this is probably designed to put Leesa at ease and not for my personal benefit.

I'm awkwardly trying to introduce Nadia to Leesa. "Ah, Leesa, this is Nadia…she is my favorite waitress, a friend really, she works at the Broadway Deli in Montrose."

"Nadia, this is Leesa. She is here from Vancouver. She was my roommate in college." *When will Nan realize I have no idea why Nadia is here? My God, could they be on a date?*

"I asked Nadia to come here tonight because of her involvement with Darilyn," Nan eventually clues me in. "I hope we can unravel some of the mystery surrounding Ms D'Angelo tonight and hopefully find her and Ginger safe together somewhere." This sounds a little cryptic to me but I am willing to do whatever I can to make this work.

"Leesa, why don't you start by telling us how you met Ms D'Angelo and what happened in Vancouver," Nan says amiably as she quickly turns on her tape recorder.

"I met DeeDee at the Women's Community Center. I think it was the middle of the summer, August or maybe July." Leesa looks at me as though apologizing for some indiscretion before continuing. "A lot of women go to the Center just to meet other women, but all kinds of women go there."

"Wait a minute." Nan turns off the tape recorder. "I'm sorry to interrupt you so quickly but are you talking about Darilyn now?"

"Oh, sorry. She wanted us to call her DeeDee…like her initials. Darilyn D'Angelo. Something about the repetition strengthening her cosmic power."

"Oh. Go ahead, please. You were saying something about all kinds of women...?"

"Yes, there are many straight women there also. Single, married, and divorced, mothers with young children. Free childcare is an important component in the success of the center. There is something for everyone. New Age spirituality is the backbone of the center. Last year everybody was reading *The Da Vinci Code* and before that *A Course in Miracles*.

Nadia looks unhappy or maybe just disappointed at this. "So the Center was primarily a religious institution?"

"Oh, no, not at all. Women come to swim, walk, run, and hike. There are softball, soccer, and football teams too. We celebrate Solstice but also secular holidays."

"How did you and Darilyn actually meet?" Nan stands up and walks over to the bookcase where there is a framed photo of Ginger and me at the camp grounds.

"I love to go to plays and concerts and there was something at the Center at least once a week I wanted to see. I noticed her sitting near me on the floor at a Holly Near concert the anti-war coalition presented. We started talking about the war and Holly Near songs we both loved."

Leesa takes a deep breath before she continues. "We went out for tea after the concert and became lovers that night." Now I knew what the apologetic look was for, but I am beginning to wonder where this is going.

"Can you tell me what actual involvement Darilyn had with the Center?" Nan wants to keep this on track but Leesa is having trouble getting to the point.

"She volunteered to teach a Goddess Spirituality class and asked me to help her recruit students for it. One of the art classes last year painted life size murals of the Goddesses for some class room walls, so we went there first. It was easy to interest those women in her classes." Leesa continued, "The Community Center assigned a room for our use on Tuesday and Thursdays from six till ten. The art classes donated hand made clay sculptures of the Earth Mother, and women from the literacy groups brought posters with poetry by Maya Angelou and Dorothy Allison to create the proper ambience."

"How did you get from a class on Goddess Spirituality to being involved in a secret lesbian society?" Nan prompts.

"DeeDee talked to us about her experiences living in Africa. She lived and worked with Dagara tribal women for two years. The first step to membership is to accept the belief that there is a deeper power in the universe and that we can tap into it. If anyone admitted they did not believe that, Darilyn invited them to leave. She did not try to convince anybody."

I have been watching Nan as she listens intently with a bemused look. She is so totally in charge when she is working on a case, it is difficult to remember she is also the Nan I bowled with at the 8 Mile Bowling Alley before it was torn down. The Nan who made me eat buffalo burgers at her 4th of July Bar-B-Q's. The Nan who kissed me at midnight in 1987 at Laverne and Shirley's New Year's Eve party and forgot to stop for several wonderful minutes while Auld Lang Syne played.

"Did anybody actually leave?"

"Oh, yes. A few traditional Catholics couldn't agree that human beings have any personal spiritual power and left. Gradually the group got smaller as certain issues began to polarize various groups of people. The happily married women were the next to go.

Darilyn helped those of us who remained develop our own power rituals and ceremonies. Once we had our own rituals, we made the decision to close our meetings to the public. If anyone wanted to observe a meeting, they had to make an appointment.

When we got down to a small core group, Darilyn started to talk about the rituals and sexual customs." As we all looked expectantly at Leesa, she cleared her throat trying to find the right words to continue.

"Women do not sleep with men. Instead they choose to sleep and live together to empower themselves to be able to meet with men on an equal basis. A member can choose a woman within the circle as her lover and she becomes her life partner. After this, she is not allowed to make love to another woman. If she does, it is believed her partner will die and she will be considered her murderer."

At the word "murderer," we both looked with some surprise at Leesa. Nan starts jotting notes in her book again. Suddenly self-conscious, I clear my throat nervously and wait for someone to say something.

Nadia looks around the room for approval from someone to speak. Leesa slightly shrugs one shoulder and nods her permission for Nadia to take over. "That is the same thing Darilyn was talking to us about here."

"What are you talking about? You didn't tell me anything about murder." I can't believe Nadia is saying this. Nan gives me a tight lipped warning look, which I take to mean, "Shut up."

The story Nadia tells us answers many of our questions.

"I first met Darilyn even before she opened the restaurant, even before she bought the building. It was the beginning of March, the first time she came into the Deli for lunch. You may remember that week; it was when the terrible snowstorm caused so many schools and businesses to close. She made quite an entrance, dressed all in red with huge white snowflakes plastered to her red angora cap and long dark curly hair. She was laughing, as though walking through a blizzard to get to a deli was a great adventure, and everyone in the restaurant felt lightened that day by her free spirited attitude towards the storm.

"That afternoon, she sat for three hours drinking tea and eating grilled cheese sandwiches with kosher dill pickles while she talked to me. One by one, all of the other customers left and still we talked. She wanted to know all about Montrose and all about the Deli. When she announced she was thinking about moving to Montrose and opening a vegetarian café here, the other waitresses stopped by her table and told her some things that they had never told me. Kim's brother was out of work and was an expert house painter. Ruth wanted to go back to school to get her degree. Something strange happened that afternoon. As we watched the whirling snow outside the windows, the feeling of confinement seemed to bring us close."

Nadia stands up and paces around the living room, not meeting anyone's eyes as she talks.

"Before she left, she asked us what the date was," she continues. "When Ruth told her it was March 4th, Darilyn laughed and said 'Of course it is. How perfect! This is the omen I have been looking for. I will move here and I will open my café here. March forth, the one day of the year that is a mandate for life.'

"After that, we all became friends. She called us her three musketeers. I introduced her to Mr. and Mrs. Cohen and they loved her. I know she told them she would never ask any of us to work for her. She called that poaching and said it was against her ethics. Mr. Cohen in particular was impressed with her credentials from Provence and her tenure at the Globe in London. He introduced her to his realtor who arranged the purchase of the old building on the corner. It was a dairy when I went to high school here. The renovations were done quickly. She said she already knew exactly what she wanted."

Abruptly, Nadia sits down and starts looking through her purse that she has left on the chair closest to the door. "I have some notes here that I took at one of our first meetings that might explain a secret society better than I can."

She started to read to us from the small spiral notebook. "A secret society is an organization of chosen persons whose members, purposes, and rituals are kept secret. The initiation typically begins with an oath pledging secrecy of all the proceedings of the society and assigning special obligations to its members.

"The Hung Society of China, a secret society of women, lasted over 1,500 years. In modern civilizations, secret societies such as Freemasonry are numerous. They offer various types of mutual aid for their members who are ill and to the families of deceased members."

Nadia closes the notebook and looks around at us. "I believed in her. I still do. I can't believe that Darilyn or the Dagara Society had anything to do with the murder."

Nan says gently, "Nadia, the murdered woman's name was Belinda Norton. The night she was murdered she introduced herself to Abigail Carr as BeBe. Her husband and parents say they never heard her use that name before."

Nan turns off the tape recorder and gets up to stretch her legs. "Do you mind if I ask both of you a few questions?" she asks Nadia and Leesa. "I need to understand what was actually going on here."

Nadia is holding her breath and nodding. I'm suddenly reminded just how young she is. Any of us in the room could be her mother.

"I did some research today. The Police Captain in Vancouver gave me certain signs to watch for with secret societies. I'm not saying they are all dangerous or even illegal, but as Police Chief I need to know what we are dealing with here and we're running out of time"

Nadia helps me take empty cups to the kitchen while I put on a pot of coffee and make some fresh tea for Leesa before we settle down to listen again.

Nan looks grateful for the fresh mug of steaming black coffee I hand her and continues, "A key marker is that secret societies invariably create a public face that does good works. We know that Belinda Norton was a large contributor to a lot of political charities. Does anyone know anything about Darilyn's charities?"

Nadia promptly answers, "Darilyn was planning to donate a large sum of money to build a Women's Community Center here in Montrose, similar to the one Leesa told us about in Vancouver. She said she was meeting with women in the community to see if there was popular support for it."

Nan seems to think this is very important. "Do you know who she was meeting with? Where?"

The tears Nadia has been holding back all night start to escape one by one. "I promised not to discuss any of this."

Nan nods her head thoughtfully but replies firmly, "Nadia, there has already been one murder. I need your help."

Nadia tries to wipe the fat tears away with a tissue I've pulled from my pocket before they reach her mouth. "I know you are right. Darilyn talked to all of the women who owned businesses or worked on 9 Mile Road. Maria Morgan from the Italian Gardens was one of the first ones but Maria didn't have any interest in anything Darilyn tried to talk to her about. Maria thought Darilyn was coming on to her."

"Who did have an interest?"

"I don't know for sure. Darilyn didn't tell me everything but I know she spent a lot of time with China Jane and Tootsie Siegel. Oh, and she used to go into Mr. and Mrs. Goodnights pajama store and talk to the woman in there. Several teachers and the principal from Montrose High are regular customers at Vegelina's, and they often left together after Dagara meetings.

I have to ask her. "Nadia, what about Ginger Harris? Did Darilyn know her? Was Ginger a member of this secret society?"

"No, I never saw her at any meetings but I think Darilyn wanted to meet her. I saw the name Ginger on Darilyn's calendar and asked her about it. She laughed and said I was a silly jealous schoolgirl. She told me she needed to remember to buy some ginger for an apple tart she was going to make as soon as fresh apples were available."

Nan asks her if she can remember what day of the calendar she saw Ginger's name on. When Nadia hesitates, I pull the flat calendar off my desk to help Nadia visualize where she may have seen it written. She easily points to the top row, right hand side. Thursday, Sept 7!!!!

Nan glances at her watch as though time is running out. "Nadia, is there a secret core group that may know more about Darilyn's plans? Or where she might be? I need to know where these meetings are held."

Leesa interrupts, "Nan, in Vancouver, a few of us went away alone several times. The other members did not know about it. DeeDee said it was important for small groups of women to spend time alone away from their communities participating in group rituals. The time alone and the rituals were supposed to help us bond. We selected a female father figure to go with us and give us her male energy to balance our female energy."

"A female father figure? Do you mean they use a woman who looks masculine for their rituals? It sounds kinda kinky to me, Leesa. I like butch women as much as anybody, but not as a father figure. That's sick." It's impossible for me not to get into the conversation although I can feel Nan glare at me when I keep interrupting.

Leesa patiently tried to explain. "It is not a sexual thing, Carla, although sometimes it turns out that way. The ritual helps women find their own male energy. Balancing the yin and yang is one way of saying it. It's not natural for either party in a sexual union or in matters outside the home to be only passive. Woman to woman sex as equals is considered normal, as are all other forms of sexual expression."

"The most masculine looking women I know are Shirley King and Frankie," I speculate. "I doubt if either of them is involved in this. This is not Frankie's style."

Nadia's voice is soft as though she is hesitant to express her opinion on masculinity. "What about China Jane? I know Darilyn spent a lot of time with her. Mr. Cohen said she looked like his favorite pitcher, Al Kaline, when he saw her going to a game one day with her Tigers baseball cap on."

"You are right, Nadia! How could we have overlooked her? Now, there is a woman who can keep a secret."

When Nadia and Leesa are finished talking, I ask Nan to step outside the back door with me while I let Skip out. "I'm pretty sure I know where they are," I start. "I didn't know if I should say this in front of Nadia or Leesa." It's colder out than I expected and Nan pulls me back into the kitchen while we wait for Skip to finish patrolling the yard. "Any reason you don't want to say it in front of them?" she asks more or less rhetorically. We both know she is in charge here and I will follow her lead without too much hesitation. I'm excited by my theory and I have a strong feeling that I am right about this.

Nan, Nadia, and I talk about my ideas while Leesa stifles a yawn and listens quietly. After I unfold an afghan on the couch to cover Leesa with, I start. "It's seems obvious Darilyn was going to attempt to recruit Ginger for this secret cult. And Darilyn must have already known Belinda, maybe for a long time since Belinda was calling herself BeBe."

Leesa is nodding her head in sleepy agreement and snuggling deeper into the throw pillows under the afghan.

"So anyway," I continue, "I think Belinda Norton and even Ginger are somehow involved with her. Or they were involved with her. They may have been planning to go away for a woman's retreat and something went wrong. Belinda was the only one who was married. What if her husband found out and killed her in a moment of jealous rage?"

"What I would like to know is if Darilyn and Belinda were a couple." Nan looks at Nadia, as if she might know. "DeeDee and BeBe seem to be quite a coincidence. What would happen if one of them was cheating, and the other one found out?"

I said, "We know Belinda gave Abigail Carr a ride back to her hotel the night she was murdered. I doubt if that interlude was platonic. Is it possible Darilyn found out, killed her, and has disappeared on her own?"

"Darilyn is not the violent type, I know she wouldn't kill anyone" Nadia still wanted to believe in Darilyn.

"I keep thinking about the cars. One track mind, you know. Darilyn's and Belinda's cars were parked side by side Friday morning behind Darilyn's restaurant."

"Your point is?" Nan must be playing the devil's advocate. She knows the point better than I do. She just wants to hear my theory out loud.

"If Belinda drove Abigail to Dearborn after the reading, why did she come back to Montrose? Did she go into the restaurant expecting to meet Darilyn? If Darilyn killed her, which I doubt, why didn't Darilyn get in her car and drive away afterwards?"

"None of these theories can hold water if we don't also consider Ginger. What part does her disappearance have in this?"

"Okay Sherlock, let's hear it. Where is Ginger now? That is what we need to know. I don't want another woman turning up dead." Nan doesn't sound impressed so far.

Just as Nan says the word "dead," her pager and cell phone ring at the same time. "Lawson here. That's right. The MacArthur Bridge? Is the Harbor Master there? Put him on, I want to speak to him personally. Have you notified the Wayne County Medical Examiner? Give me twenty minutes, I'll be there."

"Carla, will you take Nadia home for me? I'll be in touch." She is out the front door and pulling out of the driveway in her unmarked basic black Ford Crown Victoria in less than thirty seconds.

Leesa, Nadia, and I look at each other as if a tornado has just swept through my house. Nadia says she needs to get home. Her mother is watching her little girl and Nadia has a nine o'clock class in the morning.

Leesa wants to stay at my house and get some sleep. She has been up almost twenty-four hours and jet lag is catching up with her. Darn skinny vegetarians! They have no stamina.

Skip and I drive Nadia home in silence. When we pull up in front of her house, there are no lights on. "We'll walk you to your door," I offer, hoping Skip won't bark and wake her neighbors or her mother. After a second's hesitation, she leans over and gives me a sweet young girl kiss. "G'night, sweet dreams," she teases as she jumps out and runs to the door.

I sit there for a minute totally dumbfounded, and then realize I better drive away before she comes back, or worse yet, her mother comes out of the house with a shotgun.

BJ Brown
Vietnam
1967–1968

When I arrived in CuChi, I found living conditions very different from Qui Nhon. The base was a mosquito infested complex of Quonset huts. Nurse's quarters, called hooches for some never explained reason, were crawling with roaches. I missed my old bed; the one assigned to me here was a steel cot that was several inches too short for me and surrounded by thick mosquito netting.

Tiny gecko lizards squatted in the mud along the dirt pathways surrounding the outdoor showers. The shower floors were slippery with frogs just out of reach of the cold water. I hated using the outhouse in the middle of the night; any sudden barrage of artillery fire would cause my heart to hammer nearly as loudly as the guns.

My assignment was the emergency surgical team, on call twenty-four hours. Our working environment was wretched. A primitive blood stained tent, worse than the tents I had imagined before my first days of active duty, was used for surgery. We didn't have nearly enough supplies. During emergency surgery, we shared instruments with no time to sterilize anything.

The hospital was severely overcrowded, not only with American GI's and South Vietnamese soldiers, but also with North Vietnamese military and Viet Cong POWs. Many of the severe casualties we treated came from a wooded area less than ten miles from the base where the fighting was always intense.

We lived daily with the constant threat of attack from mortar shells, rockets, and even hand gun fire. When we heard bombs and land mine explosions nearby, we prayed for the daily convoy from Saigon to arrive safely. The trucks delivered our medical supplies including penicillin and the blood we needed for transfusions. Ironically, the US government considered both blood and ammunition Priority One Cargo.

Land mines exploded daily, which discouraged any exploration by ground troops of the area. Any nurses assigned to combat duty were considered non-expendable personnel in Vietnam. Our commander interpreted this to mean nurses must be driven everywhere. He would not permit our lives to be risked in helicopters. The rules bore no resemblance to our reality in CuChi. The chances of a jeep hitting a land mine were much higher than the odds of being shot down in a slick, the name we called helicopters.

The US constantly bombed the nearby forest and sprayed thousands of gallons of Agent Green on it in an attempt to defoliate the area and flush out the bands of guerilla fighters. It wasn't working. By the end of 1967, I had been at the base for four months and things were getting worse.

I had a few days off planned for Christmas that year. Qui Nhon seemed like home as much as anywhere, so I caught a ride back to the hospital there with a medic crew on a slick. I figured I could always help in the surgery, or Mama Tuyen would take me in for a few nights. Peggy was still there but Janice had gone home. Her bed was still empty so I bunked with Peggy Christmas Eve. We both got drunk and cried. It felt good.

I remember telling her she was the sister I never had. She told me how much she missed Janice.

Tuyen, Ly, and Lanh were glad to see me. As soon as Lanh knew I would be staying for a few days, he started baking. He asked me what my favorite Christmas treat was but I couldn't remember anything but fruit cake. After Christmas dinner, he proudly brought out a chocolate birthday cake so we could celebrate the birthday of Jesus. There were many aunts, uncles, and cousins there that day and although most did not speak English, my high school French helped me communicate with them.

That evening Tuyen asked me about my life in Cu Chi. I tried to minimize the danger so she wouldn't worry about me. Mama Tuyen had family members that lived there and although most of the Vo family was Vietnamese, some of the older generation still considered themselves Viet Minh.

I found myself on my second Christmas away from home listening to stories about the history of Vietnam and their long struggle for independence. I wondered how much the commander of our camp knew about the area our base was on.

Tuyen reminisced about the 1940's. "Twenty years ago our people were fighting for Vietnamese independence from the French. I was a young bride and both my husband and father were Viet Minh resistance fighters. The resistance forces used a system of underground shelters to hide from the French occupation army. The shelters in those days were little more than large holes in the ground covered by a trap door and camouflaged by dirt and leaves."

Lanh continued, "Many Vietnamese people forgot about the shelters, but when American planes started dropping bombs on the villages of CuChi five years ago, the survivors again went underground. While the young men are fighting above ground, the old men, women, and children are continuing to excavate the shelters. Now there are tunnels reaching all the way to Saigon."

I looked at Tuyen in amazement. "Did you help dig the tunnels?"

"No, it was too hard for an old woman like me, and I didn't want to help the Viet Cong."

I was confused and asked, "So the tunnels are only used by the North Vietnamese and Viet Cong now to fight the US troops?"

A young woman I didn't know spoke up, and Lanh translated for her. "My family lived in the tunnels. We were safe there. Every day my sisters and I used very small hand shovels that the women in my family used for gardening to dig out the clay soil. We filled reed baskets and passed them from woman to woman until they reached outside. The children dumped the soil into craters left by bomb blasts. Now, the tunnels join many villages throughout the province."

"But how could you live underground? Why didn't the tunnels collapse when Americans brought in tanks or when a bomb hit the area? How could you breathe?" I wondered if this was some sort of myth or folk tale, they were telling me.

The same young woman continued, "The ground there is hard clay which is why the tunnels do not collapse. The upper layer of soil is thick enough to support a large tank. Thousands live underground. There are kitchens and even schools for the children now. It is a living space for many families. The Viet

Cong built baffles so they could hear troops approaching and helicopters landing nearby. They also built smaller air vents for fresh air and vents for cooking smoke."

A handsome man who was holding her hand wanted me to know something, and he asked Lanh to translate for him also.

"It is very dangerous for you in CuChi province. Many Viet Cong soldiers are under your military base and perhaps even your hospitals. You must be careful at night. The VC come out of trap doors and fire AK47 rifles at anybody they see. They make bombs to throw. They help the villagers, but you are right. The tunnels are there for weapon factories, and there are many booby-traps which will kill anyone who tries to enter."

Lanh saw the look on my face and correctly interpreted it. He told the guests I was tired and Ly showed me to our room. If the story about the tunnels was true, it explained so many things. I wondered why these people had told me this.

Before I left the next day, Tuyen told me if I was ever in trouble to use her name and it would bring me help. We both laughed when she reminded me that Tuyen means Angel, and I assured her if I ever needed an angel that she would be the first one I called.

I returned to CuChi still not sure what my role in the war was. No matter how many soldiers I helped, RJ wouldn't come back. No matter how many soldiers died, I still had lost my only brother. My parents had lost their only son. Mimi had lost her only love.

One night, Viet Cong commandos, armed with AK-47s and flaming home-made bombs, blew up the Army hospital a mile away. As if in one of my nightmares, the monsters unspeakably gunned down patients as they tried to escape the burning buildings. **"Didi! Didi!" the patients and medics called to one another. "Flee! Flee! Leave rapidly!"**

Within minutes, I heard the medic choppers roaring through the dark night sky and over the thatched hospital Quonsets. They were so loaded down with wounded that, as they landed, the crews were screaming at us to get the casualties off faster so they could fly back to get more. It was near midnight, and the floodlights made the landing zone look like a scene from Dante's Inferno. The nightmare continued as burned and bleeding men on stretchers everywhere shrieked and moaned. Some cried out for their mothers. The air stunk of blood, burned hair, and melted flesh. A young male nurse near me vomited and went back to shooting morphine into soldiers who would be dead by morning.

We left the worst burn victims on the floor because it was the coolest place. I remember kneeling with a pan of cool water when suddenly the ammunition depot went up, and then there were two secondary explosions. Units of blood and surgical instruments were dashed against the walls, the glass in the windows shattered, patients were blown out of their beds, and we were blown off our feet. A 122 mm rocket came screaming in through a hole in the wall. The last thing I can remember clearly, as I fell was the feeling of my brain shifting in my skull.

Star Bright, Star Light

Carla and Skip McCarthy
Montrose
Tuesday night/Wednesday morning September 12–13

Dinah sometimes has a mind of her own, and this time she takes us back to the 9 Mile Road parking lot in Montrose instead of home. It's too cool to have the windows down, so Skip's doggy smell fills the front seat. He's sitting still on the old Indian blanket I've reserved for his use, but he is panting a little to let me know he's ready to get out of the car. The parking lot is nearly empty again tonight. A few overflow cars from the bar next to the Drug Mart on Woodward are huddled at the far end of the lot. A large white delivery truck is backed up behind the drugstore ready to unload as soon as the store opens in the morning. The driver is probably asleep in the cab.

If I am going to sit here any longer, I know I am going to have to let Skip out. This surveillance thing is my idea, not his. I put his leash on, my keys in my pocket, and get out of the car to walk around to the passenger side and open the door for him. Recently I've had to lift him down. I don't know if it is the 14 years or the extra ten pounds he has put on recently that is slowing him down. No more jumping in and out of cars for the old boy, but he still loves to go for a ride.

He seems very interested in smelling the parking lot and finds a couple of French fries to eat that the birds missed, but since there is no grass, he is going to keep holding it unless we cross the street. There are no lights visible from My Sister's Books at two in the morning, so we edge toward the meager glow coming from a night light at the Hair Boutique. A slight autumnal breeze reminds me of "cool night air like Shalimar," and I suddenly wish I were home in my own bed listening to Van Morrison.

While Skip is sniffing around in the shadows, I peer into the windows of the salon. It is spooky with all of the dolls everywhere posed like real people. It looks as though the shop is full of small customers, sitting very still under huge mounds of hair. My imagination plays tricks on me, and in the gloom, I think I can see Ginger sitting in the third chair. My attention is so focused on finding Ginger that at first I don't notice Skip giving a low warning growl.

Some one has been standing motionless in the shadows of the doorway between the salon and China Jane's. I have no idea that I am being watched until I look to see what Skip is pointing out to me. My heart is choking my throat, and I have to stop breathing for a moment to readjust. I stay very still for long seconds while the *knowing I am in trouble* feeling crept through me.

When the man turns towards me, a feeling of relief quickly rushes over me when I realize it is Pete Brown.

"Oh, it's you! My God, you scared me, Pete!" I take a step towards him and almost let go of Skip's leash. "What on earth are you doing here in the middle of the night?" My relief is full blown but my curiosity is still unquenched.

"Not working on the story alone in the middle of the night are you, McCarthy?" Pete's voice is cold, as though he is angry at me.

"Well, yeah, Pete, you know what a hard worker I am." I try to make a signature Carla joke but my uneasiness is coming back.

"You still curious about the padlocked door?" Pete's hands are in his pockets. He must be as cold as I am.

"I just know that Ginger did not disappear into thin air. Her car was right there in the lot the night she disappeared. I've got a hunch that Tootsie or Jane may have seen something."

A sorrowful look crosses Pete's face for a minute. By now, Skip is whining—I don't know if he just wants to continue our walk or if he is feeling my anxiety. Something is wrong here. I bend over to pet him and slip him a treat from my jacket pocket. While my eyes are on Skip, Pete whips his black watch plaid scarf around my face and neck. He twists it the same way my Mother twisted the ends of my headscarf behind my head into a knot on cold winter school days. The scarf is wide enough to cover my nose and mouth, but I can still see. As he pulls it tighter and tighter, it burns my throat as it squeezes out my breath. There is a sickly sweet smell like cheap varnish. Things are going around and around in black spirals, and if there are any lights on the way I don't see them.

The last thing I can remember clearly, as I fell is the feeling of my brain shifting in my skull.

Carla McCarthy and BJ (Jane) Brown
Friday, September 15, 2000 cont.

"What happened to you? Where did you go after the war?" I still had so many questions but we were running out of time.

"I had a severe head injury when the rocket blew up in our infirmary. There were so many people injured that night. Not only in the field, but patients from other hospitals, our own personnel. When our building caught on fire, someone dragged me unconscious out of the flames and through a nearby trap door leading to a medical room in the tunnels. I never found out who did it, but they saved my life. A Vietnamese nurse there happened to be a member of the Vo family. She took care of me and somehow got word to Mama Tuyen I was alive and needed help.

"I spent ten years in Vietnam after the war working in the orphanages. Working with the children helped ease my anger and depression. They were good years for me.

"After my grandmother died, I lost track of my family and Mimi. When I got back to the States, curiosity led me back to Michigan. I went back to the old neighborhood but there was no one there from the old days who remembered me or my family except Patty Clark. We had dinner and promised to keep in touch.

"After that, I traveled around the country like a vagabond for a long time. I settled down for a few years in California when I met someone and thought it might be time for a home and life of my own. During those years, I thought I was ready to be plain Jane for the rest of my life. Barbara Jane was a daughter, a sister, a sister in-law. BJ was a soldier, a survivor. It was time to see what just plain Jane could accomplish. I went to school and renewed my nursing license. Rachel and I had a nice little house in Bakersfield, with orange trees in the backyard. I loved the smell of the air, the birds singing in the trees.

"I liked cooking and we opened a small Chinese restaurant. I could only be happy so long before something would go wrong. I tried, I really tried, but I admit I was moody and I drank too much. I blacked out one night and when I came to, Rachel had a broken wrist. Within a week, I found a VA rehab center in Arlington and was on the road again. When I left, Rachel hired two of Mama Tuyen's nephews who had immigrated to the United States. I knew she could trust them and within a few years, we owned three restaurants in central California. I told Rachel she could have my half of the money, but she kept making deposits every month in a bank account for me.

"There were some bad years after that I don't want to talk about or even remember. VA hospitals would always take me in when I hit bottom.

"In Chicago, I got a job working in a Chinese restaurant, and I finally felt like I knew what I wanted to do. When the owner wanted to retire and go back to China, Rachel sent me $25,000 and I put a down payment on the restaurant. I had a one-room apartment and worked seven days a week for a year.

"Eventually, another Vo nephew moved to Chicago and took over the restaurant for me. Since Rachel had been banking one half of the proceeds from the restaurants for me for years, I suddenly found myself with a lot of money. I added her name to the deed for the Chicago location of Tuyen's, and now we owned four Chinese restaurants all managed by Vo brothers.

"I knew Mama Tuyen would be happy the Vo family was so successful in America.

"I came back to Michigan for my mother's funeral. I was in Vietnam when my grandmother died, and no one could reach me when my father died. When Patty Clark phoned me in Chicago about my mother, I knew I had to come home for her funeral.

"It was the right thing to do."

Carla McCarthy
Montrose
Wednesday, September 13, 2000

When I wake up, I feel like I have been sick for a very long time. I am sore all over and my right hand feels as though it is on fire. I try to move it some place cooler before I realize my hands are tied tightly together in my lap.

Skip! Where's Skip? I'm sitting on a cold slab of concrete. The wall pressed against my back has a damp winter chill. As the fog starts to lift, I remember what happened. Pete! Pete did this to me. Why? What is going on? My thinking process is so fuzzy I wonder if I've been drugged. This feels like a bad drunk, which I gave up for this very reason. Where is my dog? I'll never forgive myself if anything has happened to him.

At first, it is too dark to see anything, and I drift in and out of consciousness. The sound of thunder wakes me up. Reality returns at dawn when a little bit of light sneaks into the room. I can see I am in what looks like a poorly organized storeroom. Boxes are everywhere along with folding chairs and a putrid smell that is a mix of soy sauce and mildew.

A shapeless lump moves under a blanket in the shadows. The legs protruding from the mound look like Pete's and the shoes confirm it. Pete is sitting across the room from me slumped sleeping on a cardboard box. A gun within reach of his right hand is in danger of sliding onto the floor.

"Skip!" I try to call, but my throat is so sore it comes out as a croak. It is loud enough to wake Pete, and he looks around as though he doesn't remember where he is.

I struggle to sit upright but the effort makes my heart pound. "Why, Pete? Where is Ginger? Did you kill Belinda Norton?"

"You shoulda minded your own business, McCarthy," he muttered almost incoherently. "My mother…" His hands covering his face muffle his voice so I am not certain what he is saying.

"Pete, please untie me. My hands are numb." I can't believe Pete means to hurt me and my philosophy has always been to ask for what I want.

"Shut up! Shut up! You damned women...all of you. This world would be better off without you fucking dykes! You ruined my life! I'll get rid of all of you if I have to." He pours something out of a Coke bottle onto his scarf and heads towards me. For a second I remember the smell; it must be what he used on me in the parking lot.

"Wait a minute Pete. Tell me what happened. What are you so angry about?"

"You want to know why I'm pissed off? I'll tell you. Things are all backward in this country now. Women are making the big bucks, driving the fancy cars...thinking they are men. Women have no use for men anymore...that's not right. I read those wild hearts ads...women looking for women. My mother was fine until she started answering those phone calls at the paper."

"Pete, you wanted to run those ads. They brought a lot of money into the paper. We can stop running them. I never thought your mother should have to take those calls."

"That's not the only problem my mother has had since my aunt came back. You would have thought she was my father come back from the dead. Just because she looks like him, she was trying to be the boss of the family, doling out allowances to my mother and me, asking me what I was doing with my money, how I was running the paper."

For once, I was speechless. I didn't want to make him any madder than he already was.

"I saw your slutty friend Ginger pick you up for lunch in her new Lexus. She didn't earn the money for that car, I looked her up, her family has big money and that wasn't good enough for her, she had to go work at that lesbian bar so she could meet more women. I'm a man, I shouldn't have to drive an old car that is falling apart, I shouldn't have to take the pitiful leftovers you lesbians don't want."

"Pete, you didn't hurt Ginger did you?"

"She came over here sniffing around my Aunt Jane. Now she is not going to leave until I get some money."

"Is this what this is all about? Money?" I was trying to put the pieces together. His aunt? He mentioned his Aunt Jane; could China Jane be his aunt? There is a family resemblance that I would never have seen without a clue. They are both tall and have a similar rangy build, but Pete was darker like his mother. But why does Tootsie look so much like Pete's mother? Does he have two aunts?

"That's what everything is about, isn't it? I asked Angela out, did you know that? Your little intern friend. She turned me down, said she didn't date anyone she worked with. But, she didn't turn you down, did she Carla? I saw her getting in your fancy car after work. You were probably showing off your car to her, weren't you? You always pretend you are so broke, but I know you still get royalty checks from the book you wrote. And what about your blueberry farm? All I hear about is how good blueberries are for you now. You even wrote an article about it and I let you put it in the Times. I'm sick of you making a fool of me."

"Pete, that is not true. I have never tried to make a fool of you. I admit we disagreed about some things but I always liked you. Remember how we used to sit around eating cookie cigars and making jokes about Bill and Monica?"

"Oh shut up! Just shut up! I need to think. I can't miss this opportunity. Ginger has money, Darilyn has money. They are not leaving until I know I have enough money to leave town. I've got to get away from here."

"Pete, you can let me go. I'll loan you some money if you want to leave town, and I'm sure Ginger will too. Let's end this before someone else gets hurt." I still don't know how Belinda fits into this but I don't want to mention her.

"How do you think I feel? My Mother has turned into some kind of freak. When Aunt Jane bought the restaurant, I thought things would be better for us. We could be a family again."

"So, China Jane is your aunt? Why didn't you ever tell me? She and I played softball together; she is a very nice woman."

"My mother started staying out every night and never had any time for me anymore. So I came over here to talk to Jane a couple weeks ago, find out what was going on. I saw my mother sitting in a booth with her; she had on a red wig and make-up. She looked like a whore down on 8 Mile Rd."

"I had to be sure it was her, so I followed her when she left the Times. It didn't take me long to figure out she was masquerading as Tootsie Siegel. That was her maiden name, you know. Jewish. We are Jewish, nobody knows that. Since my grandparents died, I have tried to forget it too."

"Pete that is nothing to be ashamed of. It sounds like your mother was just trying to run a hair salon and make some extra money."

"Don't give me that naïve act McCarthy. She is sleeping with my father's sister. When people find out, I will be the laughingstock of Detroit. None of this is my fault. My mother and Jane invited those two rich dames here. I saw my chance to make some money. With enough money, I can forget about this town and make a new start."

"Pete, untie me and we can go to my ATM and I will give you some money and you can leave town right now. I don't have a lot but I can send you some more when you get settled."

"The police are going to think I am the one who murdered that woman. I didn't but I know I will get blamed for it. I can't face that, I can't go to prison. If I let your friends go, they will go straight to the cops."

"Pete, let me go. I'll get you some money. I promise I won't go to the cops. You can get out of town and then I'll let Ginger and Darilyn go when you are far away."

"I want to trust you McCarthy, but I know you won't be able to resist writing about my family. It's not right. You women will all stick together. Everything is all fucked up now."

Pete stands up suddenly and the gun falls to the floor. It doesn't go off and I wonder if it is even loaded or if he used the last bullet on Belinda.

"Just be quiet McCarthy or I'll have to drug you again. I need to think, I'm going upstairs."

I looked around, trying to see a way to get out of here. The room was dimly lit by a 60-watt light bulb attached to a cracked ceramic fixture in the ceiling. Six white molded plastic lawn chairs are arranged in a semi circle under the hanging bulb in the room farthest from the stairwell. An antique love seat is pushed against the wall with a floor model ashtray next to it. Ginger is curled on one end of the couch with her head on the armrest. She's not moving or talking but I know it's her. A chill touches my shoulder blades and makes me think for a moment she is dead. I shake it off and tell myself she is sleeping. Pete may have drugged her with the same nasty stuff he knocked me out with.

"Carla McCarthy? Is it you? Can you get us out of here?" A weak voice comes from somewhere in the room but it takes me a long moment to see a body lying on the floor near the hallway.

"Yes it's me, are you all right? It's okay, Pete has gone upstairs. How did you get here?"

Darilyn sounds more alert now that she knows someone is here with her, "I came over to see Jane and Tootsie after work, I was supposed to meet Belinda here. When Jane left to look for Belinda, Pete came in and knocked me out with something."

From upstairs a door creaks open and footsteps can be heard descending the stairs. The door opens and Pete slips quietly back into the room. I'm shivering uncontrollably both from fear and from the damp chill in the air. He takes a seat in one of the plastic high back chairs in the center of the room and waits. Ginger still hasn't moved as far as I can tell. Darilyn seems to still be in the same position. I try to remember how long they have been missing but my head is pounding with such intensity I am having trouble remembering.

A dim light goes on at the top of the stairs and a woman is standing there who looks vaguely like Tootsie without a wig.

"Pete, let's go. I'm ready." Her voice sounded lifeless and tired, not at all like Tootsie. Before I can get a good look at her, the light goes out and Pete quickly starts up the stairs.

Carla McCarthy and BJ (Jane) Brown
Friday, September 15, 2000 cont.

"Is that when you saw Mimi again?"

"The day of the funeral was more surreal than anything I had experienced in CuChi. The aunts and uncles I remembered had died and my cousins had taken their place in the family. I wouldn't have known them if I had passed them on the street, but here I could see a family resemblance. Average, white Americans with a touch of Missouri pride. Different on the outside from the Vo family, but not on the inside.

"A short, gray haired woman and a tall, handsome, younger man were edging closer to me before the service. Mimi looked even more different after thirty years than I would have expected, but somehow I knew it was her. The young man holding her arm had to be Peter.

"When he got closer to me and I could see his face, a hot flush rose to my cheeks, and I was afraid I was going to faint. If RJ had lived, this is what he would have looked like. My baby brother, grown up. Peter's hair and eyes were darker and he didn't have Bobby's infectious grin, but there was no doubt he was my nephew. Guilt, love, sorrow all flowed over me so strongly and for a long moment I couldn't breathe. What had I done?

"After the service, we rode together in the limousine provided for the procession to Sunset Hills.

"They were strangers to me, but they were family. Mimi was no where to be found. Everyone called her Miriam or Mrs. Brown. It didn't feel right. Mrs. Brown was supposed to be my mother. I was amazed to hear Peter talk about my mother as Grandma Brown. He told me he cut her grass and she taught him to play Monopoly.

"I moved back to Michigan. Rachel had married long ago, and the Vo brothers were taking good care of our restaurants. It was time for me to make amends and start a new life.

"I bought a house near Mimi and her son and tried to be a sister-in-law and aunt to two strangers. Mimi bore no resemblance to the fun loving laughing girl I knew from my own childhood. I started calling her Miriam and she didn't object. When I brought a bottle of wine for dinner one night, she rather angrily refused. She and Peter did not drink or smoke. Theirs was a Christian household, she adamantly told me.

"It wasn't long before the old urges came back and I went looking for a cooking job. I needed something to fill my hours while Miriam and Peter were at work at the newspaper. I was overjoyed when I found a small restaurant for sale in Montrose. It was connected to a vacant storefront and I planned to expand if I could get a liquor license.

"My new family resented the fact that I was spending money to purchase an old building. They thought it was folly, a waste of my meager savings. For some reason, I had not told them how wealthy I was. Years of being alone and keeping my personal business to myself, I guess. Anyway, I started to realize how much in debt they both were. I wanted them to buy some new clothes and I offered to buy Peter a new car. He took the money but he wouldn't tell me what he spent it on when he kept driving his old sedan. I knew he wanted a new one. I saw him looking at the Cadillac and Lexus ads in the Sunday papers. I told him about the Corvette my Dad brought home in 1953 and we all were amazed when he looked it up and found out what it would be worth today. He seemed to think it should have been part of his inheritance. Too bad my parents sold it after RJ died, before my Dad knew Peter was on the way. I was the one who loved cars but my Dad wanted RJ to have it.

"Soon after that, they both started coming to me for money. I told them I was very willing to help them, but I needed to know more about the finances at the paper. I was trying to take RJ's place as the head of the family. Peter badgered me to tell him about his father and what our childhood was like. In hindsight, that is when we all should have gotten some sort of family counseling. There was so much guilt and resentment among us that none of us knew how to handle. Peter started asking me why I had never come home to visit, why our family was estranged for so many years. I didn't want to answer and I resented his pressing me.

"If only I had known how bitter he felt and what hostility was building up in him, maybe I could have prevented what happened.

"The restaurant kept me busy during the day, but I started to get lonely and bored. Miriam was happy if I would sit and watch television every night with her, but I was used to more freedom. I joined a softball team and met other gay women. I also became friends with Laverne and Shirley at the bookstore.

"I was restless. Eventually, I started going to a gay bar I read about in a tabloid I picked up at My Sister's Books. It was a good place to drink and meet people. I don't believe in coincidences, but it was the same bar where Ginger Harris works. I think that may have been where I met you, too, Carla.

"Looking back, I realize I had a big crush on Ginger for a long time. She never told me about Frankie. I was spending several nights a week at the bar, which was not a smart thing for an alcoholic like me. It was not hard to resist a drink when things were going good, but later on, it proved impossible for me.

"Miriam was becoming more possessive. She wanted me to come to her house for dinner every night. When I told her I was busy, she started reminding me of the summer she was a newlywed and she cooked for me. She would say hurtful things about how hard it was to be a widow and how lonely she was. I asked her why she didn't marry again and she actually said, 'Two loves in my life were enough.' I wondered who the two loves were and if one of them was actually me, but I was afraid to ask then.

"I came out of the bar one night about midnight and saw Mimi sitting in Pete's Saturn sedan at the back of the parking lot. She must have known I saw her because she followed me back to my house. We had an argument that ended with her crying and admitting she was confused about her feelings for me. She wanted to know if we could get back together. I told her we had nothing in common anymore; I saw her only as my nephew's mother now.

"There was nothing left of the Mimi that RJ and I had loved. I was probably too harsh that night because that was the beginning of Tootsie, although I didn't realize it at the time.

"The next day she had calmed down and seemed to accept the fact that there was no future for us. Instead, she had a business proposition for me. She wanted me to rent the other half of my building to her for a hair salon.

"I tried to talk her out of it but she wouldn't take no for an answer. 'Surely, your cosmetology license has expired. You don't want to go back to school now, do you?'

'That license is just a way the government has of taking your money, but I can pay a fat fee and renew it, if you think that is important.' Mimi answered.

'Miriam, you are out of practice. You don't even do your own hair any more.'

"I was afraid to look at her when I said that, her gray hair was so aging and the style looked like a pixie cut from the fifties. I wonder when she gave up her beautiful long curls.

'It's like riding a bike; once you learn you never forget it. I am tired of you calling me Miriam; I'm tired of being Miriam. I'm going to call the beauty shop Tootsie's'

'Styles have changed a lot since the sixties.' I reminded her.

'Oh, no they haven't. Hair dressers today are just lazy. Women still want perms and big hair; they just can't get it from Lazy Sam's and Bald Rick's.'

'You crack me up, but you may be right. I don't know anything about hair-styles, I just know about cooking. But one thing you can't deny, you won't have many hours to work if you insist on staying at the Times with Pete five days a week, eight hours a day.'

'I'll make a lot of money on Saturdays and I'll sell and style wigs. That will be my specialty. I can work on the wigs at home after the shop closes. You have your precious restaurant; I should have my own business, too.'

"I had no answer to that so I set up a $10,000 bank account for the Hair Boutique in her name and told her that she would have to buy all of her equipment and pay her expenses from that. I would not give her any more, but I wouldn't charge her any rent. She stayed busy remodeling the empty space for the hair salon for a while, and I thought the crisis was over.

"One night at Les Girls, I saw an attractive woman come in who seemed familiar. Long, dark brown hair and eyes with beautiful long, black eyelashes. She was dressed in a flamboyant fringed shirt and three-inch high cowgirl boots. She had a toothpaste-ad smile you usually saw only on television. I thought I saw her looking at me, too. Before I could make my way across the dance floor, she was gone.

"Miriam's car was in my drive when I got home that night. I wasn't ready for an argument. I'd had a few beers and I just wanted to go to bed. When I made the decision to go in, she called my bluff. When the familiar knock came at the door, I had to let her in.

"She won and I lost, but I can't blame her. We both wanted her to be some-one I could love and I think she wanted to be someone she could love too. The woman with the makeup, perfume, and high-heeled boots was Miriam.

"We both knew the innocent Mimi could not come back and now Miriam was leaving too. Tootsie Siegel was the new owner of the Hair Boutique and my new lover. She started using her maiden name, Siegel, and made me promise to help her keep her new identity a secret from Peter.

"My behavior became as irrational as hers. The truth is, we both were a little psycho. She became obsessed with money. She was always coming up with some impossible scheme to get a lot of money. I foolishly promised her when the time was right I would help her.

"I do blame Darilyn, though, for starting this. When she first came to town, she was very friendly with both of us. Tootsie and I spent hours with her talking about politics, spirituality, and the state of our country. Darilyn is a very shrewd observer of people. I think she saw our weaknesses better than we did. Don't get me wrong, I knew something was wrong with Tootsie, but I thought with time and love I could help her.

"When Darilyn started telling us she wanted our help to build a Women's Community Center in Montrose, we were intrigued. She confided in us that she had $250,000 to get the project started. I did not tell her I had any money, but offered to help her with fundraising. The hope that young women would have a chance to explore all of their opportunities in a safe environment was very appealing to me. When I left high school, there were no role models in the lesbian community. My life, and maybe Mimi's, would have been different if we had a place to go to meet other women like us.

"Tootsie maintained her Mrs. Brown persona and kept working at the Times with Peter during the day. She spent the evenings and Saturdays dressed as Tootsie and worked at the salon. We always had to sneak around so Pete wouldn't find out. I confess I found her attractive and enjoyed being with her but I wasn't used to living with so many secrets.

"Darilyn, Laverne, and I became great friends. We had our businesses in common to talk about and we daydreamed about a utopian community. Darilyn used Laverne and me for her own purposes, but we weren't innocent either. Laverne loves Shirley and is very dedicated to her, but they were having problems. I still loved Mimi, but Tootsie was different. I guess the best way to explain it is that Mimi was the kind of girl you married, but Tootsie was the kind of woman you would have an affair with. I know that sounds awful, but it is true.

"The three of us spent a lot of time talking about a women's secret society and how we would run it. It seemed like an erotic fantasy to me, and I didn't believe Darilyn was serious when she asked me to be the father figure in a ritual she was planning. Tootsie and Shirley knew about the plans for a Women's Community Center but they had not been told yet anything about the secret Dagara rituals.

'The problem was, I didn't realize how damaged I was. I thought I was the strong one, but the shrink who came in to see me when I was arrested told my attorney that I have a severe case of Post Traumatic Stress Disorder. It is especially severe because of the stress of my brother's death before I even went to Vietnam. Being with Tootsie triggered memories of RJ, and it is even worse now than it was when I first came back to the states.

Darilyn, Jane, Ginger, and Tootsie
Montrose
Thursday, September 7, 2000

"Oh! Oh! Is that Ginger sleeping on the couch? What did you give her for dinner?" Darilyn asked Jane as her eyes accustomed to the gloomy room.

"Looks like too many carbs to me. You didn't feed her moon cakes did you?"

"Sh-h-h-h! No sense in waking her up. That's the problem, we were talking and drinking, and I totally forgot to offer her any dinner. She's going to have one hell of a headache when she does wake up. I made my special recipe Long Island Ice Tea; if you are not used to drinking it will knock you on your butt. I thought she could handle it."

Darilyn noticed Tootsie coming out of the store room, "Hi Tootsie, have you been here long?"

"I just got here a few minutes ago, Thursday night I work late." Tootsie looked angry, as though she was suspicious of Jane's explanation of her sleeping companion. "Everybody knows I work late on Thursdays, so they can do whatever they want."

"Where's Belinda, I thought she was coming with you tonight? We have a lot of plans to make for the retreat." Jane asked. It was becoming a problem to get everyone together at one time.

"She was supposed to be at the restaurant as soon as the First Thursday thing was over. She just had to go see that Brit. When she wasn't there by ten, I thought she might have come straight here." Darilyn sounded annoyed when she answered, which was very uncharacteristic of her when she talked about Belinda.

"No, we haven't seen her tonight. You probably just missed her. Did you drive over?"

"No, I walked and I left the back door open. Damn, now someone is going to have to go look for her."

"Why don't you call there and tell her to come on over?" Jane was getting tired and it showed in her voice. "And tell her to hurry. I want to get this meeting started. If we don't, Ginger won't be the only one sleeping."

"I don't believe you said that—if you want to sleep with Ginger, why don't you just admit it?" Tootsie looked at Jane with a challenge in her eyes that Jane had never seen before. It upset her more than she wanted to admit in front of Darilyn.

Darilyn tried to ease the tension, "She wouldn't answer the phone even if I did call. I left her a note and told her to wait for me; I said I'd be right back."

Jane was embarrassed for Tootsie and just wished the night were over. She was getting one of her rare tension headaches and she was afraid she might lose her temper with her.

"Look, I'll walk over there and collect the lost, little rich girl and bring her back, okay? I need some fresh air and everybody here should just cool off, too."

Darilyn said, "Better take a jacket, it's cooled off a lot and it feels like it is going to rain any minute." Jane grabbed her Detroit Tiger windbreaker and her signature red baseball cap without comment and bounds up the stairs with none of Darilyn's hesitation.

Carla McCarthy and BJ (Jane) Brown
Friday, September 15, 2000 cont.

"Jane, I'm fascinated with this story but what really happened to Belinda Norton? The Daily Inquirer ran a copy of the Dagara Creed that was found in Darilyn's private office at Vegelina's and insinuates Belinda's death might have been a ritual murder.

"Was she being punished for cheating, why was she naked?"

"Carla, I don't know why she was naked. I've thought about that so often. She must have been expecting Darilyn and was planning a surprise for her. I was angry when I left Tootsie and Darilyn and tired, too. I remember feeling irrationally irritated with Tootsie for being so irrationally jealous of Ginger but I was also angry with myself for having to deny the attraction I felt to Ginger. She seemed so fresh and uncomplicated; I admired her because she was so obviously comfortable with who she is.

"Confused thoughts were chasing around in my head." *Why couldn't Tootsie be more like her? Why couldn't I be more like her? And why didn't Darilyn know where her girlfriend was?*

"I tried to shake it off, but my mood was getting darker and darker and I was feeling trapped again. I had a feeling Pete was snooping around my restaurant and my house.

"I never actually asked her, but if Mimi stayed home for thirty years taking care of Pete and waiting celibately for me, no wonder she was so manic-depressive. RJ was gone and I no longer wanted to pilot the Magic Carpet.

"It was inevitable that Pete would discover his Mother's new business." *If she would just tell him the truth, we could all get on with our lives. They were so locked into the devoted widowed Mrs. Brown and her needy fatherless son routine they couldn't see how sick they both were.*

"When I got to Darilyn's restaurant, it was pitch dark except for a bright floodlight above the rear door that temporarily blinded me when I looked at it.

"The lights were off in the hallway and the main dining room looked dark too, but I thought Belinda might be in the kitchen. The last thing I remember is a loud crash…it filled the air.

"Suddenly I was back in a thatched Quonset hut and a naked villager was running towards me crying 'didi didi'. I must have blacked out.

"When I woke up, I was home, in my own bed and thankfully alone. It was nearly noon and I felt terrible. My head hurt and I knew aspirin wasn't going to help this time. I called the restaurant and Hannah and Kim were there; I told them I wouldn't be in until later, maybe not at all. I drank all of the cold water in the refrigerator and several cups of coffee before I realized I needed to see my doctor. Something was very wrong and I couldn't remember what. The anxiety I felt was as bad as when I was on the road and I was afraid I had made a fool of myself again.

"My regular VA Hospital doctor made time to see me but didn't have any new answers for me. After his exam, he told me I was drinking too much and working too many hours. 'BJ, you know what your triggers are. When you are overtired and under stress you are vulnerable to these kinds of episodes.'

"I admitted to having several mixed drinks the night before but not enough to black out. 'I don't need to remind you that as an alcoholic, even a small amount can bring on an attack. I'm going to prescribe a sedative and some vitamins for you. If you can, take a few days off and go home and catch up on your rest.'

"I went home and slept the rest of the day and night. I dreaded going back to the restaurant. When I saw you Saturday, I was embarrassed and defensive. I'm sorry I was so rude. Carla, I swear I didn't mean to hurt her. I honestly don't know what happened that night."

Belinda Norton
Montrose
Thursday night late Sept 7, 2000

The big, silver Cadillac hummed as it hurried northward along the Southfield Freeway toward Montrose. Its driver tonight was even more preoccupied than usual. Her thoughts were fragmented and fraught with conflicting emotions.

I know DeeDee is going to be angry because she has had to wait for me. Serves her right, I always have to wait for her. If she would have closed up that stupid restaurant a little early, she could have met me at the bookstore and none of this would have happened.

And Jeremy will be sullen because I am out so late tonight. He'll pretend he's sleeping when I get home but I know he waits until I get in to go to sleep. He's so much like my Father. If he knew where I've been tonight, he'd have a stroke. For that matter, if DeeDee ever finds out, she will probably break up with me. She has been looking for an excuse to see other women. I know she spends a lot of time with Jane and Laverne. I can't imagine why; they are both too old for her and they are both such dykes. If I dare ask her about it, she will use the Dagara rituals as an excuse that she's looking for the father figure...

I don't care what either of them says; I wasn't going to pass up a chance to drive Abigail Carr to her hotel. She could have had a dozen women take her home but she asked me. She's probably mad at me, too. I wanted to go up to her room with her but the way we were making out in the car I knew I wouldn't be able to leave if I went in. She was so hot in the parking lot I couldn't believe it when she stripped her shirt off in the front seat. It felt like the days when Nikki and I were sneaking around and made out in the Cobo Hall parking garage before a NOW convention.

When I get to the restaurant, I'll say I have to go to the bathroom before she can start giving me the third degree, and I'll undress and come out with avocado oil all over me and let her try to catch me. That drives her crazy when we play hide and go seek and I'm slippery and naked.

Thank you, goddess, for this beautiful body you have given me.

Daily Operational Summaries for September 12, 2000
BRIDGE JUMPER OFF MACARTHUR BRIDGE—BELLE ISLE, MI
D9: Person in water (Probable loss of life)—51 year-old-male—Detroit, Mich.

Station Belle Isle received a report of a person in the water off the MacArthur Bridge. Once on scene, police were able to get inside the vehicle and retrieve a wallet with identification to be used for obtaining identifying information.

Detroit Police found a suicide note inside of Mr. Norton's vehicle. Air Station Detroit and Aids to Navigation Team Detroit conducted several sorties with negative results. Station St. Clair Shores' airboat served as a dive platform for the Detroit Police Department.

Air Station Detroit and Station St. Clair Shores performed two sorties with negative results. Dive operations will resume on Wednesday along with side scan operations being provided by the Michigan State Police. Station St. Clair Shores may assist with the dive operations on Wednesday, if requested to act as a dive platform.

Carla McCarthy
Montrose
Wednesday Evening September 13, 2000

While Leesa is making chiropractic adjustments to relieve Ginger's backache, Frankie is hovering around trying to make herself useful. She has brought over two beautiful and warm afghans that she crocheted to keep her hands busy while Ginger was missing. It feels like I will never be warm again, and I've got Skip tucked under the blue, plaid afghan with me.

Mr. Cohen has sent Nadia over with two trays of food from the Broadway, and she needs to go home soon. I know she doesn't want to leave and miss anything, but she will be back in the morning to take Leesa to the airport. The emergency room doctors have prescribed sleeping pills for Ginger and me but I'm not taking them tonight. I may never sleep again. Frankie is screening my calls. I've told her I only want to talk to Nan.

"I've been very patient, but if you are feeling okay, could you please tell us what happened?" Leesa asks as she chows down on a giant kosher corn beef sandwich. Apparently, it is not easy to find a good Jewish deli in Vancouver.

Ginger and I look at each other for approval. I know she is not ready to tell her story, and when she gives me the go-ahead nod, I start with what happened this morning. I've been replaying it in my head ever since I got out of that horrific basement. I already gave Matt Blanke at the News a sanitized version, when he called. If I can't write the story myself, he may as well.

"Thank God for Laverne. Her twenty-five years of teaching early morning classes makes her still want to get up and get going early, even though the bookstore doesn't open until ten. She was on her way into the store to do some paperwork when she saw Skip sitting forlornly in Jane's doorway. He was wet and shivering and at first she thought he was a lost dog." My throat is sore and my voice is hoarse from the stuff Pete used to knock me out with.

"I think Skip recognized her because he started whining and barking at the door asking her to let him in. She looked around for me and when she saw my empty car in the lot, she assumed the worst. She knows I would never leave my dog outside unless something was terribly wrong."

Frankie and Leesa are both staring at me straining to hear. I know they want me to tell them every little detail but I am so weary of reliving it. When I hesitate, Leesa offers to bring me a cup of tea with honey. I gratefully nod yes and close my eyes for a minute, but the picture of Pete keeps coming back. I feel like such a fool. I trusted him; I thought I knew him so well.

"Laverne didn't waste any time looking for me. She called 911 right away. Nan said she heard the dispatcher sending a squad car to the rear entrance of China Jane's restaurant." In between sips of the hot tea, I continue to tell them what happened.

"Just as Pete and his wacko mother were leaving the building through the back door of the Hair Boutique, a squad car pulled up and restrained them for questioning. The 911 call wasn't clear about what the problem was, and the officer thought they might have been robbing the hair salon. He knew what Tootsie Siegel looked like and didn't believe Mrs. Brown was the owner."

Leesa gives Skip a bite of her corn beef. He is recovering quickly now that we are home, but I was worried about him when he didn't stop shivering all morning.

"When Pete walked out, Skip flew through the open door and down the stairs barking like the Hounds of Hell were at his heels. Another squad car pulled up and the driver thought there might have been a canine problem and followed Skip down the stairs with his revolver drawn. The Chief was right behind him.

"Suddenly Skip was kissing me and Nan was hugging me right in front of everyone, although I don't think anybody noticed. It looked like she was putting her arms around me to untie my hands. My face was wet from tears and dog kisses; I think we were all crying. The officers untied everyone else and called for an EMS unit."

When the doorbell rings, it is Nan with a bouquet of flowers and a box of Milk Bones.

Documents used by the prosecution in court cases: the State of Michigan against Barbara Jane Brown, Miriam Siegel Brown (aka Tootsie Siegel) and Peter Robert Brown

"The Lesbian Spirit," *Girlfriends Magazine*, July 1994 [Re: The Dagara tribe of Burkina Faso, West Africa]: [1]

Evidence Location: Taken from basement of 15000 E. Nine Mile Rd Montrose, MI

"Nothing is truly intimate outside of ritual," says Sobanfu Somé. Sexuality, including woman-to-woman sexuality, is so integrated into the spiritual life of the Dagara that her people have no word to specify "lesbian" or even "sex." Like many other Africans, the women of Dagara do not sleep with their men. "Women need to sleep together, to be together to empower each other...then if they meet with men, there is no imbalance."

Tribal women not only sleep and live together; they join together for group rituals. "We go to a cave or bush and do rituals to build male energy. We have a female father who gives us male energy. She looks like a male. Anything we feel or experience that we haven't dealt with is expressed." This women's group ritual balances their male/female energy. "It is so we are not completely male or female."

Dagara women believe that once you've made love with your life partner in this circle, it is extremely dangerous for her to be intimate with another woman. If you break the circle, you bring in alien energy. Your partner will die. The diviner in our village comes in and says, "You murdered her"...Sobanfu also says women must look at sex as a journey. "You are traveling to a place not known by you or your partner. Only your ancestors know. When two people merge, your genealogy becomes a participant in what's going on."

Psychiatric Report
Date: September 27, 2000
Patient: Barbara Jane Brown
Report Prepared by: Dr. Nancy Kilpatrick, Clinical Neuropsychologist

This patient appears to be suffering delayed symptoms of post-traumatic stress disorder (PTSD) [2]which originated with the death of her brother and her experiences as a combat duty nurse in Vietnam. Ms Brown suffered a severe closed head injury when she was injured in a bomb blast. A Contra Coup Injury results when the brain in injured in two places.

It is difficult to predict the course PTSD. Events and people's reactions to them vary greatly. For example, an adult might become aggressive; have outbursts of anger, or experience sleep problems and nightmares. Triggers of PTSD symptoms are unique to the individual.

PTSD may develop immediately after a traumatic event for some, or months or years later for others. In Ms Brown's case, the symptoms were exacerbated when she was forced to abandon the behavioral and emotional avoidance techniques that have insulated her from her symptoms. Her interactions with Miriam and Peter Brown triggered her impaired memories. Ms Brown's anger and depression may have eventually surfaced but without therapy, we cannot be sure.

Recommendation: Within the court's sentencing guidelines, a minimum sentence with scheduled on-going visits with a court appointed psychiatrist is indicated

Psychiatric Report
Date: September 29, 2000
Patient: Miriam Siegel Brown
Prepared by: Dr. Morris Everret

This patient suffers from a borderline personality disorder. It is obvious to this trained observer that she lives in an immature psychological world, fueled by certain constitutional vulnerabilities. She has attempted to shield herself from conflict and anxiety by splitting the world into all good and all bad.

Although this may have produced an illusory sense of psychological safety, in fact, it renders relationships fragile and chaotic.

Two divergent personalities were observed in this patient using the Dissociative Interview Schedule (DDIS) testing method.

1. As Tootsie Siegel, she demonstrates a classic histrionic personality: immature, attention seeking, self centered, vain, emotional, excitable, shallow, and insincere. During this manic phase, a flirtatious and seductive side was particularly noticeable with regard to her relationship with her sister-in-law, Barbara Jane Brown.

2. Miriam initially exhibited schizoid and narcissistic tendencies with a rigid and inflexible outlook and a high degree of self imposed 'Christian' morality. This is especially interesting as Mrs. Brown is of Jewish heritage and was devoutly Jewish before her marriage to Robert Brown and his subsequent death at an early age while serving in the Vietnam War. Family, friends, and co-workers universally described her as cold and distant.

A strong trait of avoidance was also observed as the patient acknowledged her unhappiness about being alone coupled with an exaggerated sense of her own importance.

Recommendation: A plea of *"guilty but mentally ill"* is a viable option. This option indicates that the defendant was impaired at the time of the crime; it is not the same as legal insanity. After receiving this verdict, the defendant would be required to receive psychotherapy in a hospital setting.

Psychiatric Report
Date: October 1, 2000
Patient: Peter Robert Brown
Report Prepared By: Dr. Morris Everret

Most U.S. courts have adopted a broad definition of the insanity defense:

"A person is not responsible for criminal conduct if at the time of such conduct, as a result of mental disease or defect, he lacks substantial capacity either to appreciate the wrongfulness of his conduct or to conform his conduct to the requirements of the law."

Current courtroom procedures—where mental health professionals on both sides give conflicting evidence as to the defendant's mental ability—seem to confuse juries and do little to find justice.

Proving the defendant guilty but mentally ill can be done in two ways. The first option may be used with clearly psychotic defendants. The second, antisocial personality disorders—people who essentially lack a conscience, cannot be judged as guilty but mentally ill.

Although our opinion indicates that the defendant was impaired at the time of the crime, his actions do not indicate a defense of legal insanity.

Recommendation: It is our opinion; Mr. Peter Brown is competent to stand trial.

• Adapted from Atkinson, Atkinson, Smith & Bem's *Introduction to Psychology*, Harcourt Brace Jovanovich Publishers, 1990, pages 612–613.

Carla McCarthy and friends
Southfield
Saturday 7:00 PM September 30, 2000

A small dinner party at Laverne and Shirley's Southfield home is just what the women of Montrose need two weeks after their ordeal. The white tablecloth is set with white and gold Lenox dinnerware and sparkling Waterford crystal glasses. The repartee as well as the mood is light at the beginning of the evening.

Shirley asks Carla, "You remember that ditzy blond with the pink streaks that works at the Drug Mart?"

"I'm trying to forget. I guess you haven't seen her lately. Her hair is black now and the pink streaks are gone."

"Blue streaks now, I know. I did see her today. With her talent for doing hair, too bad she couldn't have taken over the Hair Boutique. Now that Tootsie Siegel is locked up there will be an empty storefront there."

Nan says, "Just what Montrose needs. Another weird hairdresser. I can just see the McGuire twins with blue hair."

"Oh, I know! One with blue and one with pink. We could finally tell them apart." Carla was happy people could laugh at her jokes again and happy she and Nan were at the party together.

"Does anyone know what will happen to China Jane's? That place brought a lot of traffic to the area," Shirley asks as she awkwardly balances a tray of spiced hot apple cider and offers it to her guests as they wait for Laverne to bring the spinach quiche from the oven.

"Jane plans on keeping it open. She hired a young woman from Vietnam to manage the place for her and she is keeping Hannah and Kim. Her doctor is testifying for her. It looks like the DA is only going after a charge of homicide," Nan says.

"She won't have to do much time. She may get off with probation and public service. Her war record will help a lot."

Shirley is showing Nan some photos. "We found a very nice condo to lease for the whole month of December in Tarpon Springs. With Ginger taking over so many responsibilities at the store, we will have a lot more time to travel."

Ginger said, "It was time for me to quit working at Les Girls. I'll be able to go to bed at a more normal time. I see what a problem alcohol was for Jane and I don't want to be part of that problem any more."

"Those same women, who came to the bar to see you, can come to the bookstore now. Think what a public service you will be performing…dollars being spent on books instead of beer!" Carla was only half joking about this. She was glad to see Ginger out of the barmaid business.

For the first time tonight Darilyn spoke up, "The Cook family is donating $50,000 for a literacy program at the Montrose Women's Community Center in memory of Belinda. That should mean a few more readers."

A chorus of cheers went up around the room but was quickly doused when the women thought about Belinda.

"I feel so guilty about Belinda. It should be me standing trial and not Jane. If I hadn't bought those knives that day Belinda might still be alive. I knew I should have put them all away before I left that night. I wanted to show off the all the new kitchen things to BeBe when she got there."

"Darilyn, believe me, this is not an interview. I'm not going to use what you say in the paper, but do you know why Belinda might have been undressed and why the new pots and pans were scattered across the kitchen floor?"

"You are not asking me anything the police have not asked me Carla. Neither one had anything to do with Jane and I'm going to have to testify about it. I hope it helps her." Darilyn said sounding abashed.

"Often when Belinda came to the restaurant after I closed, we would play an adult version of "Hide and Go Seek." BeBe made it more interesting by playing without her clothes on and with the lights out. She read my note that I would be right back and was going to surprise me I'm sure.

"As for the pots and pans, I had them stacked in a corner with the knives and she probably knocked them over, or maybe Jane did in the dark. The police thought Belinda may have taken them off the rack and thrown them at Jane to defend herself, but I had never put them on the rack yet."

Everyone was looking at Darilyn but she looked so embarrassed by her admission she didn't seem to have anything else to say. Laverne saved the day by asking Carla, "So what will you do now? Do you still have a job?"

Carla walks over to her desk in front of the windows and opens the top drawer. "Funny, you should ask," she replies as she takes out a thick folder marked "CONFIDENTIAL."

"Thanks to the Freedom of Information Act, I will have everything I need to write a book about what has happened in Montrose this year." She started taking out various files, which everyone wanted to read until they realized how long they were and how small the fine print was.

"Will we be in it?" Shirley asks rather hopefully.

"Yes, of course Shirley, all of my friends will be in it. You might not recognize yourselves, though.

"You know you must change our names to protect the innocent and the guilty," Nan thinks she is the legal expert.

Carla had been worrying about that very thing.

"What will you call it?" Laverne is still good at getting to the bottom line.

"I think I will call it "Montrose" or maybe "A Tangled Web." What do you think?"

The End

Post Script

During Jane's trial, Leonard Goldstein, her defense attorney painted a compelling picture of Barbara Jane Brown as a war hero. A selfless nurse, someone who was injured while caring for our American boys. The same boys who were sent on a hopeless mission to a God forsaken heathen nation. A woman who was willing to sacrifice everything for her country. A woman who had already lost her only brother in Vietnam. Goldstein brought in a doctor who specialized in treating victims of PTSD and it's delayed onset in many people.

Jane would not let Goldstein blame Tootsie Siegel for anything that happened. When the prosecution brought out the fact that Tootsie Siegel was Jane's sister-in-law and the two had been friends since childhood, the chatter in the courtroom caused the judge to admonition the spectators with a threat to clear the courtroom.

Women who gave their lives in service to their country deserve to be remembered.

Army

During the early morning hours of June 8, 1969, a Soviet-built 122-mm rocket slammed into ward 4 of the 312th Evacuation Hospital in CuChi, Vietnam

- Lt. Sharon A. Lane 24 year old died instantly.

Died in a plane crash returning to their duty stations at Qui Nhon from hospital duty in Pleiku, November 30, 1967.

- Capt. Eleanor Grace Alexander

- 1st Lt. Hedwig Diane Orlowski

Died in a helicopter crash near Saigon, February 18, 1966

- 2nd Lt. Carol Ann Elizabeth Drazba
- 2nd Lt. Elizabeth Ann Jones

Died in a plane crash returning to their duty stations at Qui Nhon from hospital duty in Pleiku, November 30, 1967.

- Capt. Eleanor Grace Alexander
- 1st Lt. Hedwig Diane Orlowski

Lt. Donovan, from Allston, MA, became seriously ill and died on July 8, 1968. She was assigned to the 85th Evac. in Qui Nhon. She was 26 years old.

- 2nd Lt. Pamela Dorothy Donovan

Suffered a stroke and was evacuated to Japan where she died four days later on August 14, 1968. A veteran of both World War II and Korea, she was 52.

- Lt. Col. Graham, Chief Nurse, 91st Evacuation Hospital, 43rd Medical Group, 44th Medical Brigade, Tuy Hoa, from Efland, NC

US Air Force

Capt. Klinker, a flight nurse with the 10th Aero medical Evacuation Squadron, Travis Air Force Base, temporarily assigned to Clark Air Base in the Philippines, was on the C-5A Galaxy, which crashed on April 4, 1975 outside Saigon while evacuating Vietnamese orphans. From Lafayette, IN, she was 27. She was posthumously awarded the Airman's Medal for Heroism and the Meritorious Service Medal.

- Capt. Mary Therese Klinker

CIVILIAN
American Red Cross

- Hannah E. Crews

Died in a jeep accident, Bien Hoa, October 2, 1969.

- Virginia E. Kirsch

Murdered by US soldier in Cu Chi, August 16, 1970.

- Lucinda J. Richter

Died of Guillain-Barre syndrome, Cam Ranh Bay, February 9, 1971.

Army Special Services

- Rosalyn Muskat

Died in a jeep accident, Long Binh, October 26, 1968.

- Dorothy Phillips

Died in a plane crash, Qui Nhon, 1967.

Catholic Relief Services

- Gloria Redlin

Shot to death in Pleiku, 1969.

Central Intelligence Agency

- Barbara Robbins

Died when a bomb exploded in front of the American Embassy, Saigon, March 30, 1965.

- Betty Gebhardt

Died in Saigon, 1971.

United States Agency for International Development

- Marilyn L. Allen

Murdered by US soldier in Nha Trang, August 16, 1967.

- Dr. Breen Ratterman

Died in a fall from a balcony in Saigon, October 2, 1969.

- Regina "Reggie" Williams

United States Department of the Navy OICC (Officer in Charge of Construction)
Died of a heart attack in Saigon, 1964.

Journalists

- Georgette "Dickey" Chapelle

Killed by a mine on patrol with Marines outside Chu Lai, November 4, 1965.

- Philippa Schuyler

Killed in a helicopter crash into the ocean near Da Nang, May 9, 1967.

Missionaries

- Carolyn Griswald
- Ruth Thompson
- Ruth Wilting

All three killed in raid on leprosarium in Ban Me Thuot during Tet February 1, 1968.

- Betty Ann Olsen

Captured during raid on leprosarium in Ban Me Thuot during Tet 68. Died in 1968 and was buried somewhere along Ho Chi Minh Trail by fellow POW, Michael Benge. Remains not recovered. Listed as MIA.

- Eleanor Ardel Vietti

Captured at leprosarium in Ban Me Thuot, May 30, 1962. Still listed as POW.

- Janie A. Makil

Shot to death in an ambush, Dalat, March 4, 1963. Janie was 5 months old.

- Evelyn Anderson
- Beatrice Kosin

Both captured and burned to death in Kengkok, Laos, 1972. Remains recovered and returned to US.

Australian Nurse Corps

- Barbara Black

Barbara died at Vung Tau, Vietnam in 1971.

Operation Babylift

The following women were killed in the crash, outside Saigon, of the C5-A Galaxy transporting Vietnamese children out of the country on April 4, 1975. All of the women were working for various US government agencies in Saigon at the time of their deaths with the exception of Theresa Drye (a child) and Laurie Stark (a teacher). Sharon Wesley had previously worked for both the American Red Cross and Army Special Service. She chose to stay on in Vietnam after the pullout of US military forces in 1973.

- Barbara Adams
- Clara Bayot
- Nova Bell
- Arleta Bertwell
- Helen Blackburn
- Ann Bottorff
- Celeste Brown
- Vivienne Clark
- Juanita Creel
- Mary Ann Crouch
- Dorothy Curtiss
- Twila Donelson
- Helen Drye
- Theresa Drye
- Mary Lyn Eichen
- Elizabeth Fugino
- Ruthanne Gasper

- Beverly Herbert
- Penelope Hindman
- Vera Hollibaugh
- Dorothy Howard
- Barbara Maier
- Rebecca Martin
- Sara Martini
- Martha Middlebrook
- Katherine Moore
- Marta Moschkin
- Marion Polgrean
- June Poulton
- Joan Pray
- Sayonna Randall
- Anne Reynolds
- Marjorie Snow
- Laurie Stark
- Barbara Stout
- Doris Jean Watkins
- Sharon Wesley
- Rhona Marie Knox Prescott

Third Field Hospital, 616th Clearing Company, 85th Evac, ANC

Sources
Vietnam Women's Memorial Project (Military) and
A Circle of Sisters/A Circle of Friends (Civilian):

Vietnam Women's Memorial Project

Endnotes

1. In the Dagara tribe of West Africa, women are valued as the source of the world's wisdom. They are valued as dreamers, as diviners, as the backbone of the community—the core of human survival. For more information please see Women's Wisdom from the Heart of Africa by Sobonfu Some

2. 3.6 percent of US adults ages 18 to 54 (5.2 million people) have PTSD

    30% of those who have spent time in war zones experience PTSD.

    One million war veterans developed PTSD after serving in Vietnam.

978-0-595-38745-8
0-595-38745-4

Printed in the United States
87215LV00007B/48/A

9 780595 387458